GETTING UGLY

by

MIKE MCCRARY

GETTING UGLY copyright ©2013 by Mike McCrary

Cover art by JT Lindroos

All rights reserved.

GETTING UGLY is a work of fiction. Names, characters, places and incidents portrayed in this book are either products of the author's imagination or used fictitiously. Any resemblance to actual events, locales or real persons, living or dead, is entirely coincidental and not intended by the author. No part of this publication may be reproduced, or stored in a retrieval system, or transmitted in any form or by any means, electronic, mechanical, photocopying, recording, or otherwise, without express written permission from Mike McCrary.

For you, you and you…but not you, asshole.

GETTING UGLY

PART I
fuck you, grande ugly.

1

Leon.

The man you'd rather be, or be with, depending on your preference. Twenty-five, whip smart head, with a body crafted from Hanzo steel. Leon could very well be the spawn of an aggressive mud pit baby making session involving Han and Hope Solo. He's nothing like that pansy Skywalker. Leon used to like Luke. At one time wanted to be Luke. Hell, he *was* Luke one Halloween. Most days his features are just shy of perfection—even his minor imperfections are considered ruggedly handsome in most circles—but not today.

That was a long time ago, long before the events of today.

His time spent with the FBI has served him well. The hours working the Bureau's program have transformed him into a perfect physical machine. Not like the beefy boys of Venice Beach. No chest shaving or sweating through black and gold spandex just so he can look sweet in a pair of smiley face boxers. He looks nice in his boxers—boxer briefs actually—but that is not why he does it.

Getting Ugly

He's not out to impress, not trying to snatch up ladies. He has a wife he loves dearly, and that's more than enough for Leon. From the moment their eyes locked over a keg of Milwaukee's Beast at Dusty Ballard's house that summer, Leon knew she was the one. Still is. That was the summer before senior year. It's clichéd, he knows, but it's the truth: when you fall you fall, no matter when it is. What can you do? So, no, he's not killing himself at the gym, perfecting himself physically, to pull in some strange while out at Buffalo Wild Wings.

No, his body has been carefully honed for endurance and—if need be—fast, effective violence. The days and nights spent working through the different regimens, the grueling federally funded training, is all for days like today.

Leon didn't use profanity for the majority of his life, considering it a simple language for simple, weak minds. But days like today have forced Leon rethink that philosophy.

Today Leon thinks, *Fuck Luke*.

Today those good looks hang from his bones like a shirt draped over a fat boy's treadmill. Today that cut from steel body resembles a turd that's been stepped in.

Haggard.

Beaten.

Of course, Leon never thought there would be days like this. No one does. Why would they?

He sports a bulging blood clot over one eye, a deep cut seeping above his brow. Crimson strands of saliva string from his bottom lip. Sleep's a distant memory and Leon fights to stay focused, his mind drifting to thoughts of his wife—the way a child might cling to happy thoughts after waking from a nightmare. No lullaby here for Leon, only "Enter Sandman" as performed by Satan's garage band.

He stumbles through the dirt streets of Shit Town, Mexico. He's not sure of the town's actual name. His thoughts are starting to run together. Leon was given an assignment and began tracking this deranged man in LA. Then his quest took him to Chicago, and then to a tiny pothole in West Virginia. From there it was the Caymans (*That was nice.*), Warsaw (*Not so nice.*), Bangkok (*Just flat-out fucked up.*), and finally here, somewhere in the mountains outside of Mexico City.

But this man, Leon's target, is here.

He knows it.

Unmistakable signs are all around and cannot be ignored. Most notably, the swirling atmosphere of complete chaos. Behind Leon, a tiny town burns, small houses lit up like campfires. Dead bodies litter the dirt road, shell casings scattered amongst the pooling blood. An axe is planted in the chest of some poor soul. A goat runs like hell.

Leon's standard issue Glock 23 hangs in his chewed up excuse for a hand. A few locals from the town huddle behind him as if he's their only hope. Leon can't even begin to worry about them. Not because he's an unfeeling bastard—he wishes he could help—but because of the cold hard facts of the situation.

Leon can't do a damn thing for them.

He's tried before.

There was the guy at that Thai place in downtown Chicago who was kind enough to provide some useful information. Leon tried to help him.

Jesus, what was his name?

Getting Ugly

Leon struggles to remember. He does, however, remember that Thai Place Guy got up to go to the bathroom and was met by a dark stranger. Thai Place Guy received a lethal knife wound for his trouble, the blade starting at his navel and then ripping up to his sternum. Thai Place Guy's special reward for assisting the FBI? He got to watch his guts spill out over the urine-stained linoleum of a men's room. And Leon doesn't even want to think about what happened to that family in Poland who talked.

The FBI appreciates your sacrifice.

There are other helpful dead bodies scattered around the globe. The sum of those dead innocent people (well, some not so innocent) has caused Leon to think perhaps he shouldn't be so damn chatty with folks.

He pulls his cell while limping down the Mexican dirt road, his bloodied left leg dragging behind him. A torn Britney Spears t-shirt provides a makeshift tourniquet. Leon spins through his contacts and makes the call. After a one-ring pickup Leon spits out, "Cooper, I did it. Got a location on him."

Leon can't help but think back on the day he first sat down in Cooper's office.

That was two years, five months, eight days ago.

A lifetime ago.

2

Leon recalls the office being drab, sterile as hell, but with a magnificent view of the Los Angeles Westside.

Behind a cluttered oak desk sat a warhorse of a G-Man: LA Special Agent-in-Charge, A.L. Cooper, a living, breathing legend with thirty plus years on the books. The multitude of Cooper stories echo throughout the halls of the FBI. Cooper had worked offices across the U.S., as well as joint CIA gigs around the globe, and had his pick of offices years ago. After a fraction of thought he selected swimming pools and movie stars. Of course he did. It's fucking seventy-two degrees and sunny three hundred and fifty days out of the year and, oh yeah, everybody's beautiful.

Even the homeless are fives and sixes.

Cooper needed to find a good man to track down a bad problem. He'd poured over the stack of potential candidates, and most of them didn't amount to a thimble full of warm cat piss.

One, however, caught his eye.

This kid, Leon, had only been on the bureau's roster for a couple of years, but it'd been an impressive couple of years to say the least. The kid reminded Cooper of

Cooper. They shared a similar blue-collar, lower-middle class upbringing, Cooper born and bred in PA with Leon growing up in OH. Both played football. Cooper an All-District middle linebacker, Leon an All-District ball hawk of a safety with great run stuffing skills. Leon went from Quantico to a field office, then quickly made it onto a FBI SWAT team in Dallas. Currently the kid was with the Tactical Section / Hostage Rescue Team (TS/HRT.) Just like Cooper's path years ago. In fact, Cooper was on the original TS/HRT team established in 1983 for the Los Angeles Olympics in response to that unfortunate shit that went on in Munich.

The major difference between Cooper and Leon?

Cooper had the benefit of a good, stable home. Leon, on the other hand, was raised in foster homes around Ohio. Cooper guesses Leon's parents bought it in car crash, that's usually how they both die at the same time. He checks the file and sees they died in a company fire at the plant where they worked. Leon was six. The courts awarded some money, which his piece of shit aunt and uncle blew most of. The court appointed trust did have some caveats baked in that stated how the money was to be used "for the benefit of the child," but Aunt Josie and Uncle John-John took that to mean buying them a new house, car and stocking their bar for the apocalypse. Fortunately, there was still enough for Leon to go to college and have a bit left over. By the look of that wife of Leon's, Cooper guesses most of what was left went to the rock on her finger and a down payment on a new house. And upon further review of Leon's bank records, yup, that's it.

All of this makes Cooper smile. Orphans with dependency issues and the need to excel make fantastic recruits.

Leon sits across Cooper's desk, a clean-cut, poster child of an FBI man, nervously twisting his wedding ring.

Newlyweds, Cooper thinks. *Adorable.*

Kid kinda reminds Cooper of Luke Skywalker.

Cooper likes the kid, make no mistake, but this is an interview for a very special project, so it's imperative to be a bit of an asshole and fuck with the young lamb Leon. Establish dominance; develop Cooper as a father figure and whatnot.

"Leon. Or is it Leo? Is Leo short for Leon?"

Leon wants this assignment as bad as anything he's ever wanted. Though he doesn't really know what it is, he does know all about Cooper. Knows the war stories and the legends backward and forward. If even half of them are true, he wants to grow up to be Cooper, or at least his version of Cooper.

Leon fights back the nervous energy. It's okay to show respect, but mustn't show any form of pussy tendencies. "Leo would only be losing an "n" so it's not really— Leon is fine, sir."

"Fuck it. Why the FBI?" Cooper fires back. What the kid says isn't nearly as important as how he responds. Does he freeze up? Shift in his seat? Or, Godforfuckingbid, start to sweat and stammer like a five year old ballerina.

Leon wants to impress. He thinks about how all great careers start with something like this, a defining moment. One of those points on the graph that signals an upward trend, heading for the stars, knocking a big assignment out of the park, blowing expectations out of the water.

But, damn it all to hell, Leon does not know how to answer Cooper's question.

"Sir?"

"Why. Did. You. Join. The. FBI?" Cooper presses. "You wanted to expand the cock n' balls via the Glock n' badge?"

Leon's response is nothing but free-flowing youthful sincerity. "I wanted to do something, you know, something good. Be proud of my job; be proud in general. I've got friends who jumped to Wall Street. Some became lawyers, chasing paychecks. Slaves to a salary…"

Cooper slices the air with his hand cutting him off. "Right. Right. Right. Enough, son. You already got the gig, stop the shit."

"No. No shit here, sir." Leon tries not to bounce up and down in his seat. *Did he say I got the gig?*

Cooper takes a moment to chew on the honest, wide-eyed little boy look plastered all over Leon. He remembers looking at the world through that lens. That was a long time ago, and Cooper knows that world view simply does not exist—never has, never should. Cooper briefly entertains the idea of not allowing Leon to go through with this assignment. Save the kid from himself. Cooper allows a moment of silence to hang in the air while he lets his eyes tell him what he needs to know about Leon.

Is the boy completely full of crap?
No.
Will he survive?
Doubtful.
Do you have a choice?
Nope.

Cooper picks up Leon's file. "You come highly, highly recommended. Rising fast. Knocked the piss out of the test scores."

Cooper continues reviewing and discussing Leon's off the chart abilities: Leon rapid firing, speed loading, and ripping targets on the firing range to nothing before the instructors could begin to process his skill level; Leon tearing through the obstacle course like it wasn't even there. He was driven beyond reason, passing fellow cadets like they were disinterested sheep.

Leon's first day on the street?

He hunted down some stray dogs the FBI had eyes on, a beefy motorcycle gang that was selling meth to anything with a heartbeat. Leon ran up against two tatted-up Neanderthals who laid down some serious firepower with modified assault rifles—crazy, urban warfare shit. Very sophisticated for bike riding tweekers. Leon crept up behind the beasts, dove through the air, and tackled them both to the street like he was Riggs in *Lethal Weapon*. In a blink of an eye, Leon had disarmed them both and was on his feet, Glock leveled at their skulls.

"People still talk about it," Cooper wraps up with a swig of coffee.

"Thank you, sir."

Cooper glances at Leon as if trying to communicate with his mind. *Last chance to run, kid.* Leon doesn't receive Cooper's telepathy, only wants to devour whatever information Cooper has thrown his way.

Cooper shrugs. *Fuck it then.* He leans forward and gets to the meat of the conversation. "This is a man hunt. The man? Possibly the single most terrifying thing ever rendered by sperm and egg. Goddamn horror show who will kill and rob anything breathing. I need a young, aggressive agent with a healthy set of nuts. Most people are afraid to touch this shit show. You one of those homos?"

Young Leon wants to do well, excel, exceed. "Healthy nuts, yes. Homo, no."

Cooper hands Leon two, three-inch thick files. "Find this man. Bring him in to answer for the wicked he has done." Disturbing, gristly photos spill out from the files. The files have only two words on them: *BIG UGLY*

Leon lets a smile crack. He's heard stories about Big Ugly, the white whale, the Big Foot of the law enforcement community. Leon blurts, "Yes, sir." If he'd taken a moment from his race to impress Cooper to actually stop for a breath and look over the file, he wouldn't be smiling or thanking anybody for shit.

He'd bolt for the door and apply to the nearest grad school.

Cooper knows this, but he also knows where Leon's head is. He knows Leon's type: a young, strong kid who's blinded by a mix of ambition and cotton candy idealism, coupled with a not so great childhood. That cocktail has made and broken many a good man. Cooper feels some annoying need to offer a bit context. "Now, some consider this a fool's errand given who we're talking about. The levels of violence and so forth. It may take you some time. Might have to track this horrific cocksucker for months, maybe years. Can you do this for me, for the FBI?"

Leon doesn't even pretend to think about it. "Absolutely, sir." He smiles huge, completely forgetting about his wife, the one who will be left alone during

Leon's crusade. Cooper cracks a half-smile. The death of idealism always hurts Cooper.

It'll pass.

That fateful day in Cooper's office is now in Leon's rearview.

That was then.

This is now.

Leon's mind whips from that trip down memory lane to the present—his situation is problematic, at best. Today, Leon is beaten to hell, standing in the middle of a Mexican war zone.

He repeats firmly into his cell, "Cooper?"

Leon hears Cooper take a deep breath and then give an obligatory dramatic pause. He can almost see Cooper's shoulders shrug. The pause drags out for what seems like days.

Cooper finally says, "It's over. I'm being forced to end the hunt."

Disbelief rockets through Leon.

Cooper's words hit him like a spike puncturing his heart, draining his will. Hearing this news could only be matched by phrases like "inoperable tumor" or "no choice but to castrate." He feels his brain slosh inside his skull. "What? We got him. He's here. You hear me? He. Is. Here. Send in a team…"

Cooper's voice is clear and cold, as if reading ink from a page. "I want you to know, you've served the FBI admirably. Please understand, there was no other way."

"Oh bullshit…sir. I'm bringing him in."

Just before Cooper hangs up he offers, "God be with you, son. I'm sorry."

"Agent Cooper? Cooper!"

Dead air.

3

Leon slumps, his back sliding down the wall of a shack that looks like it could crumble any second. He lets his cell drop to his side, his mind a swirling wad of confusion with no direction or place to go. Leon is a man without a country, his situation as bad as it gets. No back up, and the cavalry is not coming. His mentor, his hero, his surrogate father has abandoned him when he needed him the most. He has successfully tracked down the Devil, and in return Leon's been left to tangle with him alone.

Is this what the Thai Place Guy felt while watching his guts slip from his body?

The Mexican locals scatter as if it had started raining razor blades. Leon's confusion swells as he watches the people bolt in every direction, scrambling to avoid being anywhere near him, like rats that instinctively sense the ship is sinking. *What do they know?* His stomach twists with the fear that comes from being the last to know you're completely fucked.

A fist bursts through the thin wall behind Leon's head.

Thick, well-manicured fingers wrap around the back of his neck, like a mama cat snatching up her kitten. The unseen force yanks Leon through the wall and into the dilapidated Third World home. In a single motion Leon is thrown helicopter style, arms and legs spinning. He lands in a tumble-roll across the dirt floor.

Dust dances as Leon skids to a stop. He manages to squeeze off two blind shots. Prays he hit something, anything. Nicked a vital organ…please?

Nothing.

Silence.

Tiny dots of daylight shine through the bullet holes, with thin slivers of light creeping through where the walls don't completely meet up with the roof. A cockroach sprints across the dirt floor.

A John Lobb loafer steps on the roach with a moist squish, its high-dollar companion stomping Leon's gun hand with a twisting crunch of ligament and bone. The Glock slips out from his helpless fingers. Scrambling for the gun, Leon is met with a beatdown delivered by a master of ass kicking.

A blizzard of punches, kicks, chops, flips, elbows, palms of hands—all really unpleasant shit. Leon fights back, giving him hell, but only lands every fourth or fifth fist or foot. It's not enough. Leon is fighting a beast way outside his class. Like the house of straw against the big, bad wolf, this piggy is in deep shit and sinking fast.

A Colt held by the figure shrouded in shadow jams into Leon's eye socket.

The dark figure speaks. "Hola."

Leon cannot, will not, give this man the satisfaction of knowing his fear. "Hi."

"Sucks when friends up and fuck you."

"That it does."

The dark figure readjusts his grip then continues. "What have I ever done to you? How long have you been on me?"

"Two years, five months, eight days."

"Seriously, when are you going to cease with the shit?"

"Maybe tomorrow."

"But not today?"

"Unlikely."

The dark figure playfully exaggerates a sigh then pulls back the hammer. "Buenos días, my little dead Fed."

Leon spits out a pulpy tooth. "Fuck you, Grande Ugly."

PART II
a few shitty years later.

4

It's a moist, sticky night inside a pay by the hour motel room.

Dirty, pink flowered paper clings to the walls. Even the room seems to sweat. An open window lets a breeze into this horrific excuse for living quarters. Graffiti marks the walls—something about big dicks and your mother—beer cans fill the bathtub, and what looks like old, dried-in blood stains on the carpet. A brown couch squeaks as if a jackrabbit were screwing an unwilling Tasmanian Devil.

A wiry twenty-something, Brobee is half-dressed in a *Wonder Pets!* t-shirt, camo cargos down around his checkered Vans. Brobee huffs and puffs with a much, much older hooker riding him with the enthusiasm of a comatose cowgirl.

He's working way too hard.

She's bored-to-tears.

The hooker glances at her ancient Swatch, slightly bouncing up and down. "You've got five champ." Brobee goes faster, face beet red.

The door busts open, ripped out chain lock dangling impotently from the doorframe.

Getting Ugly

Three mean-spirited gents step in. Rasnick leads the charge, with two Eastern Bloc thugs named Vig and Oleg backing him up. Brobee's eyes go wide, but keeps at his squeaky sex. He's still on the clock, dammit.

Brobee knows Rasnick is a forty-four-year-old enforcer who's gone as high as he's going on the career ladder. It probably bothers him, sure, but what are you gonna do? He does his thing, makes a so-so living, dances when the boss says boogie, and buys lottery tickets. Right now his boogie partner is Brobee.

Fucking Brobee.

Rasnick shields his eyes from the horrific intercourse as calmly he asks, "Brobee, where's the money?"

Brobee responds with hump-altered speech. "Look, Rasnick. Bro. Dude…" More squeaking. Oleg and Vig pull guns. The hooker gasps in between bounces. Rasnick's eyes never leave Brobee. "You lost twenty K on women's lacrosse."

Vig chimes in, "Who the fuck bets women's lacrosse?"

"What kind of shithead…" starts Oleg.

"That kind of shithead," Rasnick says. The room goes silent save the squeaking. Brobee is still at it. The kid's dedicated to getting his money's worth.

"Could you stop fucking her for five fucking seconds?" asks Rasnick. The squeaks stop. Bouncing hooker stops. Rasnick takes in a breath. "Tell me you have the money. Please tell me that I didn't make Oleg and Vig come down here for this sad-sack sex show."

Oleg and Vig could be twins—they're not, but they could be. Walls of former Soviet Union beef with tight crew cuts and Russian prison tats from neck to nuts. They'd joined up with Rasnick about a year ago, and things have gone well. Oleg and Vig are happy employees as long as they can drink the good stuff, get mouth-sex from time to time, and inflict pain on a daily basis.

Brobee looks over the situation and knows it's not favorable. His options are limited at best. Unfortunately, run like hell or certain death are the options Brobee usually faces. He thinks that a smart guy would find a better way to live. And he will, starting tomorrow. Tomorrow is personal inventory day for Brobee. Just gotta get *to* tomorrow, and right now that's a problem.

He tosses the naked hooker towards them with a yelp.

Rasnick and company are knocked off balance as they open fire. Their blasts crater the walls, taking out fistfuls of drywall. Brobee does a two hop, penguin walk with his cargos around his ankles. The pounding bullets barely miss as he takes a bare ass dive out the window.

Brobee hits the trash cans ass first, his tailbone screaming as his lower back locks up. He spins from the cans as Vig and Oleg hang out the window looking for a shot. Brobee manages to pull his pants up and gain speed as they open up on him. He runs like he's never run before, bare feet slapping hard on the pavement. Brobee remembers hearing something about how running barefoot is better for you, had read the first paragraph of an article about that somewhere. Thinks, *This is the start, the start of a new Brobee.*

He'll almost definitely take up barefoot running, eating right—well, better at least—and he will, without question, poke fewer hookers.

5

A cab pulls into LAX.

Brobee tosses a few bills to the cabbie. It's not enough. The cabbie screams as Brobee storms into the airport.

Always keeping his head on a swivel while he waits in line at the American Airlines ticket counter. He takes an opportunity to cut in line as the family in front of him wrestles with a stroller and three kids. At the counter a chipper ticket agent asks, "Where will you be traveling this evening?"

"Next flight the fuck outta here. Doesn't matter where," Brobee fires back as he slams down an AmEx he stole from a Persian guy he knows who churns out credit cards using stolen identities.

On the plane, Brobee starts seat dancing with headphones planted on his head, his cocktail sloshing all over his hand. He flips off the window in rhythm with Katy Perry. Other passengers pretend not to notice.

Hours later he lands at some bumfuck airport just north of nowhere. Brobee didn't even bother really checking where he was going, and he didn't recognize the name of the place on the ticket—someplace that starts with a B or an M, maybe in Montana…perhaps Idaho. He'd had to change planes three times, and he's hammered out of his skull from the Jack and Cokes.

Brobee walks through the parking lot, looking over the available vehicles as if he was shopping for a new ride. The booze is starting to fade and he lost his ticket at some point. He still has no idea where he is. Could be Oregon. Could be Canada. Could be Sweden. There are woods in the distance, with mountains. Brobee selects a slick, old school Cadillac and smashes a brick through the passenger window.

The freshly stolen Caddie weaves and winds down a serpentine, country road that's completely surrounded by thick walls of trees. The headlights cut through the dark, foggy night. Inside the Caddie, Brobee has the 10-speaker, 2 subwoofer, 200 watt sound system booming classic rock. He's enjoying Golden Earring so much he doesn't notice the red blinking fuel light.

Brobee's new ride slows down to a crawl, then rolls to a stop as "Radar Love" shuts off.

"Fuck."

Brobee exits, nothing for miles but trees, crickets and moonlight. He fumbles around the glove box and finds a flashlight. He hears a muffled noise coming from the trees far away. Distant, but it almost sounds like someone is there.

"Hello?" Brobee asks the dark.

The sound comes from deep within the woods. Brobee hates this: still half-buzzed, alone in the wild, no gas, had to bail the motel without his cell, and his only food is that extra bag of nuts he swiped from the plane. He moves into the heavy woods with the flashlight in hand.

Getting Ugly

After what seems like hours of pushing through this dark maze of bark and vegetation, Brobee's out of breath. He's been at this awhile, and hasn't begun his exercise program yet. That's tomorrow, he reminds himself as he leans on a tree.

The sound has stopped. Brobee asks, "Hello?" Nothing. Complete silence greets him from the darkness in every direction.

Dense.

Claustrophobic.

This sucks and I'm not happy.

Then the sound is back. This time it's much louder and sounds like it's just up ahead; sounds a lot like singing, actually.

What the fuck?

Brobee pushes through the seemingly endless forest until he finally reaches a clearing.

"Thank Christ," Brobee exhales. He's saved. He's so excited and happy he starts to bounce a bit. The singing continues, belting an almost operatic version of AC/DC.

Brobee strains to get a good look at something out into the distance. Something located in a large clearing has grabbed his attention by the throat. He freezes, not believing what his eyes are reporting back to his brain. He mutters to himself, "Is that? No. No fuckin' way."

Confusion fills his feeble mind as recognition shakes his flimsy body. Pure fear mixed with terror, topped off with an asshole clenching panic. Lips tremble. Eyes twitch. Flashlight drops.

He hears the sound of water trickling. Looking down, he sees piss rolling down his leg splashing all over the flashlight—so terrified he didn't even notice he was pissing himself. A new low, even for Brobee. All of this, the twitching, trembling, pissing…all of it because of what is up ahead in the clearing.

Brobee unleashes the scream of thousand girly men as he hauls ass back into the woods, running for his life. With no regard for his body, he bounces off trees, falls, skids, slides, and claws his way through the darkness, maintaining his feminine wail throughout his frantic journey to safety. Bat outta hell style, Brobee flies from the woods and lands sprawled in the road. A truck skids to a stop inches from plastering him. A portly driver steps out, but the nice guy doesn't even get the chance ask *"Are you okay?"* before Brobee jumps him. He puts a foot to the driver's balls and a knee to his chin, then steals his truck.

Brobee lets the tires peel as he continues his screaming, tears streaming and fists beating the dashboard. At the airport parking lot he brings the stolen truck to a skidding stop, leaving the engine running as he bolts for the terminal with arms flailing.

After the plane takes off, Brobee gulps down two Jack Daniel's mini bottles, skips the Coke. He sniffle-cries between breaths like a two-year-old. Far from okay, but at least he's not screaming or pissing himself. Calming down he tries to think. The wheels in his head turn as he takes a moment to piece together what he saw.

Correction.

Who he saw.

6

Brobee flies through the doors of the dark, nasty bar with purpose, ignoring everything in his path. It's a hardcore drinker's bar, where people throw a few back while minding their own business…until there's an opportunity to kill or fuck someone. A dirty mirror clings to the wall behind the bar, tattered bras hung with care like a rainbow. A burly, aging bartender wipes down glasses with a rag that looks like used Charmin. He pulls down the tail of his flannel shirt to cover the .38 tucked in his waistband.

The bartender tries to stop Brobee. "Hey, asshole!" But nothing can stop him as he burns a trail to a back room, throwing open the reinforced steel door.

He enters a room that serves both as an office and criminal playpen and finds Rasnick, Oleg and Vig playing pool. Nothing shocks these guys, but even they are a bit taken aback at seeing Brobee here.

Brobee runs toward them, forgetting these guys tried to kill him not long ago. Rasnick's punch to the face reminds him quickly. Brobee stumbles back, then tries to sooth the mood of the room. "Let me talk…" Rasnick slams a pool stick to Brobee's gut, followed by a fist to the jaw. Brobee drops to a knee and screams, "Wait!" Before Brobee has a chance to utter another word, two 9mms are jammed into his skull.

"Please listen, motherfuckers," yelps Brobee.

"Really, guy?" Rasnick slaps him.

Hammers pull back.

"I got something, fuckheads."

Earns another slap.

Oleg and Vig tighten their trigger fingers.

"I found Big Ugly!"

The room goes quiet. Oleg and Vig look to each other. They know the name, and that name scares the shit out of even them. Rasnick lowers himself to eye level with Brobee. "You mind repeating that?"

"Big Ugly," Brobee pants. "I know where he is."

"Bullshit," barks Oleg.

"He knows shit," agrees Vig.

Rasnick looks into Brobee's eyes trying to get a read. "How do I know, huh? How do I know?"

"Oh, fuck you. When have I ever lied to you…"

Rasnick slaps him again.

"Fine, fine. Okay, I've lied. But I'm telling you the truth." Brobee gets to his feet. Oleg and Vig keep their guns on his head. While adjusting his shirt Brobee unfortunately feels the need to say, "Now, if you cocksucking faggots aren't interested in finding the biggest prize on the planet, then maybe you could go fuck yourselves."

Not well received.

An avalanche of fists and feet rain down on Brobee. He's beaten to the floor, curling into a ball covering his face with his arms. This is a defensive stance that Brobee has perfected over the years. Rasnick, Oleg and Vig take turns kicking the various parts of Brobee still available.

"Stop," barks a commanding voice from a dark corner of the room.

Rasnick, Oleg and Vig follow the order, immediately pulling back as if scalded. Out of the dark wheels a man in a chair. Face covered with burns and scars, the man looks as if he was pulled from an industrial accident seconds before death. He wears a suit and tie, partly to keep a certain level of respect, but mainly to cover up his disfigured body. His legs are useless, but he opted for multiple surgeries to avoid amputation. This is fifty-year-old crime lord, Doren.

Doren eyes Brobee carefully, trying to assess if he can believe this man. "Tell me everything."

Brobee swallows big at the sight of Doren. He knows not many people actually get to speak to this man…or at least not many live after speaking to this man. He nods and begins to explain. "Big Ugly. I swear to whateverthefuck you worship, Doren, I can give you Big Ugly—spin the wheel, let's make a deal."

Doren's hard stare burns through Brobee. Bubbling rage spikes through him as Doren's memory flips through a ton of pain and unpleasantness. Big Ugly left Doren scarred from head to toe, but it's the unseen scars that truly eat away at Doren. His eyes stop just short of popping as he commands, "Call a meeting."

Doren, a king on wheels, rolls across the floor of a gorgeous penthouse hotel suite, Rasnick pushing the chair with Vig and Oleg close behind. It's a room tailored for the illusion of royalty: crystal, glass, brass, oak, fresh flowers. All at the price tag of ten grand a day.

Doren is focused, mind churning behind cold eyes that burn with a hate that few will ever know. They glide past the floor to ceiling windows overlooking the LA skyline. A family of fifteen could live here, quite comfortably. You could feed a small country for the price of the art hanging on the walls. Rasnick eyes a painting closely—he's pretty sure he can lift it out of here without a problem.

They stop as they reach a dining room that holds massive, circular granite table. Seated at the table are the other three crime bosses of Los Angeles. Knights in the round. Nothing happens in this town without these guys and Doren earning a piece of it. Outside of a random domestic violence case here and there, there isn't a drop of blood spilled in LA without these guys knowing about it. These are the lords of the city.

Cherrito: middle-aged   Latino   hood,   but worth multi-millions.

Getting Ugly

Bosko: fifty-something, full-fledged Irish mob.

Waingrow: late sixties, but tough as nails with style and class—his blue hearing aid even matches his tie.

Doren is wheeled to the front of the table, as he should be. Doren has the respect of the room and he has earned it, the hard way. Rasnick, Oleg and Vig take their places against the wall. Dorn addresses the room. "Thank you for your timely response. I called you here to discuss an urgent matter that concerns all of us. Today, right now, someone can lead us to Big Ugly."

The mood at the table turns electric, tension gravy-thick. It's as if Doren just announced that Lucifer is alive and well. Waingrow rubs his ear, adjusting his hearing aid to get it just right—wants to make sure that the guys outside got all that.

Parked outside the hotel is a standard, non-descript, trying-hard-not-to-be-noticed van. Inside the metal cube of a workspace is wall-to-wall surveillance equipment. Stacks and stacks of Federal tax dollar funded audio and video equipment. The van's interior is dark save for the bouncing red and green levels, B&W images light up the screens.

Two G-Men watch, soaking it all in. Cooper stands behind a tech, paying close attention to everything the young lad does. Shitty coffee in hand, they listen in on the crime lords' penthouse suite conversation.

Cooper's blood pressure flares at the words Big Ugly.

Over his headphones he strains to listen, wanting each and every word. He presses the headphones tight to his ears with his fingertips as Bosko says, "Big Ugly. That's a name I'd love to fuckin' forget."

The tech, too young to know what's what, asks, "Who? Big what?"

Cooper doesn't bother explaining. "Grab me a cup of coffee, would ya?"

"Cooper, you've got a full…"

"How about you get the fuck outta here."

The tech understands that. He gets up immediately, thinks of asking how Cooper wants his coffee, but thinks better of it and exits. Cooper takes a seat, and with laser focus pushes the headphones even tighter. If he could shove them into his brain, he would. He picks up a small mic that gives him a direct line into Waingrow's hearing aid; a nice link to Waingrow's head whenever he wants it.

Cooper listens in as Doren explains. "A degenerate named Brobee stumbled across Big Ugly. Simply blind luck and, after some negotiations, he has agreed to lead us to him."

Cooper speaks low into the handset. "Clear your throat if you hear me, butt fucker."

Waingrow grinds his teeth. He thinks about how long he's been at this game and never got picked up on anything. Nothing. Not one damn thing. Then, at his age no less, he gets tagged on some bullshit gambling bit. Just because some bitch got nervous and blabbed. He broke one of his steadfast rules: always pay for pussy. Paid pussy keeps quiet. But Waingrow got soft; he actually liked that waitress with the green eyes and big knockers. And what does he have to show for it? He's sitting here with these good people, people he's known forever, and he has to fuck them.

He's forced to snap out of his pity party as he hears Cooper in his ear again. "Hello, butt fucker? Clear your throat if you hear me. Butt fucker?" Waingrow clears his throat, clears his head, then says, "Think we all can agree our lives would be better if we never met Big Ugly." He hates himself, but the table bought it.

Bosko sounds off, anger-fueled tears about to flow. "Soulless, shady, fucking…"

Cherrito interrupts. "Motherfuckin' misery master is what he is. There's no God while Big Ugly roams the earth."

Bosko raises his right hand; he's missing three fingers. "Monster took my digits."

Doren regains control of the table. "True. We've all lost something to Big Ugly." Nobody there has to dig too deep to recall a *favorite* Big Ugly memory.

There was that sunny SoCal afternoon in a Ralphs parking lot when some heavy-hitting, gun-toting bad boys took down an armored car in a broad daylight. Guards were on the ground hog-tied, bags of money being thrown into a getaway van. It was an easy peasy job for Bosko's people. Until a wall of bullets carved them all to hell. Bosko's men dropped. No last words. No death rattle. Just a pile of dead bad boys. All the carnage was done by a lone, at the time anonymous, "Dark Figure" who scooped up the money bags and took off without a trace. A mysterious thief of thieves.

Then there was that time at Cherrito's little grow house outside of Manhattan Beach. He had a team of topless immigrants working day and night, surgical masks over their faces, gloves over their hands, nothing over their chests. Mixing. Bagging. Processing. A goon with a sawed-off manning the door, an accountant with an industrial money-counting machine to keep track of the stacks upon stacks of dead presidents.

Then, without warning, a knife slammed down through the top of the goon's skull, blood spurting out like Old Faithful. The accountant took a few pops to the face from a Colt. That same Dark Figure grabbed the bloodstained money, but before leaving wiped the crimson hundreds across the surgical mask and bare breasts of one of the trembling immigrants. He wanted someone to tell the tale that time. He whispered in her ear simply, "Big Ugly was here."

Waingrow tells the story of how his brother was in the comfort of his own bedroom, banging a very attractive girl who he paid good money for, when the Dark Figure showed up, stopping his brother mid doggy-style. Didn't even let the man finish. The Dark Figure handed the girl a stack of cash and escorted her to the door. Waingrow's bro tried to go at him, but he got bitch slapped back onto the bed, where he could only look on terrified, frozen by the sight of the Dark Figure holding an ignited blowtorch. He held the torch in one hand, a thick, blood-caked chain in the other. Brother Waingrow's screams echoed, his fingers gripping the mattress, chest split open and toes charred from the torch. He told Big Ugly everything he wanted, and more. Gave up safe houses, drop spots, jobs, account numbers, phone numbers, addresses…you name it. He gave up enough info for Big Ugly to sink his teeth in and really go to work. Big Ugly thanked him, and set the bed on fire.

When this conversation about Big Ugly's deeds started, the stories were deliberately spoken, clearly told. Now, they start to turn into lightning fast blips of description as floods of memories burst out—memories they've all pushed far back in their heads in order to just get through life. CliffsNotes versions of Big Ugly doing dirty deeds are spit out left and right, everyone talking over the top of one another, one sentence overlapping the next.

The time two of Bosko's best earners got cut to chunks by a samurai sword in Santa Monica.

Waingrow's Irish Bar downtown blown to shit by the rhythmic pumping of a 12-gauge in the hands of skilled killing machine. The bartender was tagged point-blank, the top half of his body found across the bar from his legs.

The chainsaw story on La Brea.

An axe was used here.

A baseball bat used there.

Hemo-soaked money shoved into bags.

Suitcases.

Trash bags.

Guns loaded… then unload.

Doren slams his palm hard to the table commanding everyone's attention. The table falls silent, all eyes on Doren as he points a finger to the burns and scars that litter his face, neck, and hands. He doesn't bother pointing out the wheelchair. "No one has lost more than me." His stare is cold. Dead. Black. The table gives a silent nod out of respect. Doren continues, "This man. This thing…" He trails off, unable to finish his thought.

Cherrito jumps in. "The last time we heard from Big Ugly, he went rip-shit fucking riot. He killed a hundred and four of our people in less than twenty-four hours. Emptied our pockets…"

"Then disappeared," says Bosko. "Went ghost. Nothing. Not one fucking blip for fucking years." He turns to Doren. "What do you propose?" Doren takes a moment, wrapped up in his thoughts. He rubs his disfigured hands across the smooth table. He can't feel it, hasn't felt anything in his hands for years, but imagines the cool feeling of fine craftsmanship along the granite. He gets lost thinking of all the things he will never feel again, all of the things that were taken from him.

Taken by that man.

That monster.

That disease.

"Doren, what do you propose?"

Doren looks up and, as calm as he can says, "Assemble a crew and execute Big Ugly."

Looks fire around the table, eyes dancing at the very thought of it. Bosko asks the question on the tip of everyone's tongue. "Kill Big Ugly? One might consider that a futile enterprise."

Cherrito adds, "Dangerous man. Not one to fuck around with. Go at him, go strong. Swing and miss… God help us all."

"Big Ugly can lay down a ton of unpleasant," agrees Bosko.

Waingrow thinks, *amen to that shit.*

Doren attempts to calm the room by breaking it down the way only a true leader can. "Vengeance is a great motivator, but should never be the only motivation. We are men of business. He took lives, but also he took assets, our liquidity. According to my accounting, he got away with just over one hundred and sixty million of our hard earned dollars. Any of you recovered from that economic setback?" Stares burn around the table.

That would be a no.

Getting Ugly

"He has to have kept that money close. We have ties at every Swiss bank, every bank in Belize, Mexico. That's too much money to not draw attention. My proposal? We each nominate some of our own to man this crew so that we are all fairly represented. Choose your best. They will go kill this man and find what's left of our money."

The table chews on that for a second. Bosko is the first to speak. "Requires a special breed."

"Requires serious loco fuckers," mumbles Cherrito.

"For incentive," Doren adds, "We give this crew twenty cents for every dollar returned to us."

From his spot against the wall, Rasnick zeros in. Something big going on behind those eyes of his, something that Doren said has set his brain ablaze.

Waingrow does the simple math. "Two hundred K per million? That'll motivate a motherfucker or two."

"With a kicker," adds Doren. "The one who puts Big Ugly's head on this table, I'll give one million personally." The criminal round table allows this to make a lap around their heads. Doren goes on. "We have to move. We have hours, not days. To put it mildly, Big Ugly is a flight risk. My representatives are ready." He motions and Rasnick, Vig and Oleg step up, looking like they could chew raw meat off the bone. Doren gives the table his final words. "I know we've had our differences, but it brings a smile to my face knowing that we can meet as men and form a plan to destroy this disease. This will work. It will work, and heal a lot of pain from our pasts. Friends, I ask you with an open heart and mind… in or out?"

Cooper cracks an ever so slight smile as he listens in on Doren's proposal. Ideas are taking hold in Cooper's big brain. A giddy feeling tingles in his stomach.

In the suite Bosko, Cheritto and Waingrow share a look.

Bosko gives his answer. "In."

Then Cherrito. "Fuckin' A Wally World, all in."

Everyone looks to the member who hasn't chimed in yet. Waingrow. He picks at his hearing aid, uncomfortable, fidgeting like a child that needs to pee.

"Jesus," Cooper says as he fumbles with the handset that provides the link to Waingrow's ear. He grips the mic and speaks as clearly as possible, explaining to the crime lord as he would an infant. "You're in. You are so fucking in. And guess what, sport, I got a representative you *will* nominate."

Waingrow shifts in his chair, hating this. Cooper doesn't care what Waingrow likes or hates. "Asshole, speak up or die in prison."

Waingrow gives up. "Yes. Of course, I am in."

Doren rubs a burn on his wrist with a satisfied grin. He was pretty sure that everyone would come to their senses, but you never really knew with this group. "I have a Gulfstream fueled and ready to go where the degenerate leads. Have your people ready in two hours."

In the van, Cooper tosses the handset, runs his fingers through his hair. His mind zooming from zero to a hundred.

Rasnick leans against the wall next to Oleg and Vig, catching his smile before it spreads too far across his face. The men in this room don't appreciate smiles from their hired muscle; they question smiles, wonder what the hell is so damn funny. Rasnick keeps his thoughts to himself, but there is some serious planning going on in his head.

8

A rundown, shitbox apartment building in the dead of night.

The SWAT team—tactical gear, laser sights, alpha dog attitudes— glides stealth-like from car to car, getting closer and closer to the apartment. A beefy team member applies a ram to the front door, which explodes into splinters. The team storms in, and muffled yells come from inside: *Motherfucker!* this and *Don't fucking move!* that. All punctuated by controlled machine gun bursts. A spray of blood splats against a window before the glass blows out, then dead silence. It's over before it started.

The SWAT team comes out spreading around high fives, yuk-yuks and fist bumps. From behind a van steps Rasnick, Oleg and Vig nowhere to be seen. Rasnick leans in and whisper-yells to two of the SWAT guys. "Buster! Talley!"

Buster and Talley, who happen to be brothers, break from the rest of the team. Talley's a 6'5" brick shithouse of a man, while Buster is a five-foot nothing sparkplug, but surprisingly strong. His lack of height, coupled with older brother Talley's defensive end body, has Buster in a classic Napoleonic twist.

Talley squints at Rasnick, then smiles with recognition. "Your case over?"

"Mom know?" Buster asks.

"No, I'm still on the job," says Rasnick.

Talley winces. "You should call Mom, man."

"Shit bro, you can't be around here," says Buster. "You get made hanging with your cop family? Not good."

Rasnick puts a hand up to stop the verbal barrage from his brothers. "Got something huge and no time." His brothers are all ears.

In a small house, their mother's house, Buster, Talley and Rasnick sit around a kitchen table, its beaten up wooden showing the signs of raising three boys. Chunks are missing, with words carved by butter knives on the top. Things like, *Buster sux*, *Talley sux dicks* and *Go Lakers*. Currently the table is home to guns, a box of Ritz crackers, a twelve of High Life, and a heaping pile of coke. Talley snorts a line, passing a pink pig shaped cutting board to Buster.

After a hard sniff, Buster grunts, "How much you thinking?"

Rasnick does the math in his head. "Even if he blew half of it, there's got to be eighty plus million. Maybe fifty on the low side."

"Fuuuuuck." from Buster.

"That's what I'm saying. I go in first with this crew. I'm so up their ass, they have no idea I'm a badge. You two show up, we dead the lot of them, grab the cash, and be done with all this low tax bracket, law enforcement shit."

Talley likes the idea, but has concerns. "That's lotto dollars, no doubt, but you're not talking about just matching six numbers man. This lotto ticket carries a gun."

Rasnick sits back, taking a swig of High Life. "Granddad, Pops, our uncles…all cops. We're stuck in a damn cycle, an endless loop. No way for this family to get above it. This how you want to spend the next twenty years?"

"Not me dog," says Buster.

Talley gets it, but he's always been the most sensible of the three. "I hear ya, man. But this Big Ugly thing? You don't even know where you're going. So how do we get to you?"

"Not sure yet. That paranoid shit stain, Brobee, he's going to search us all before we leave. No cells."

Talley thinks, then pulls a 9mm Beretta and slides it to Rasnick. "New thing. Has a GPS in the grip in case we lose it, get kidnapped or some shit." Talley's way of letting his brother know he's on board.

Buster's eyes glow like wildfire. "Fuck yes. We'll track you, roll in like cowboys from hell, and put some fire on those motherfuckers."

Talley rolls his coked-up, pie-eyes to his younger brother. "Why don't you shut the fuck up? *We're gonna roll in like cowboys from hell.*"

"Fuck you, prick."

Talley loves pushing buttons, keeps it going. "Maybe we can hold our TECs and gats sideways. Rat-a-tat-tat. Bust some caps in a nigga's ass while pumping NWA, idiot."

Buster is beginning to get offended. "Why do you have to talk to me like this?"

"You keep yapping retarded banter."

"Your attitude is horrible," Buster fires back.

Rasnick breaks it up. "Please stop." Takes a big coke snort. "We do this together, like family, and we can do anything we want for the rest of our days."

Talley lets the Buster bashing go, for the moment. He thinks, adding it all up. "Doren, those guys…they're going to know something's up when you don't come back."

Rasnick pats his gun with a grin. "I gotta plan for that too."

Buster get it, loves it. "Fuck yeah. Boom!" Snorts a line as his exclamation point. Talley rolls his eyes again, fighting the urge to lay into his brother. Calmly he says, "This crew you're going in with, what's the roster?"

"Doren has me with two standard, off the boat Eastern Bloc boys, Oleg and Vig." Rasnick goes on to describe the rogues' gallery that will make up the crew, telling the story about when Vig and Oleg unleashed on a BMW at a red light at the corner of Melrose and Fairfax one Saturday morning. They left the poor souls in the BMW bloody, mangled, twitching and flopping. Rasnick calls them the vodka and AK crowd. "They're good boys."

"Then there's the pair Bosko is bringing in," says Rasnick. "Good God." He recounts the day Bosko sat behind a desk across from Pike and Patience, both of the twenty-somethings pulsing with an unnerving, psycho-fueled energy. Still, a cute young couple though. Patience twirled a gun with her right hand, while jerking Pike's junk under the table with her left. If Sid and Nancy and Bonnie and Clyde had a foursome, these two nut jobs would be the product. Their claim to fame was this job they did where they had the tellers and customers face down on the floor next to the dead security guards, while in the back room Pike and Patience had sex on top of a massive pile of cash—actually bumping uglies on the money were stealing. They sat the scared shitless manager against the wall, apple on his head, and forced him to watch. Pike blasted the apple off of the man's head, all while never breaking is love stroke. Patience loved it. Weird sex, killing and money…that's what Pike and Patience are about. No particular order.

"Next is Cherrito's man, Chats. From what I hear Chats is, well…Chats is everything that's wrong in the world." Rasnick takes a hard swig and fills his brothers in.

Chats sat cross-legged next to a rusted bathtub in a busted up motel bathroom—a single bulb hanging from the ceiling, new level of filthy kind of place. A scar runs down one side of Chat's face, his left eye dead and glossy. Another scar runs along his neck. His chilling, rock-hard stare focuses somewhere out in the void as he tears at a grilled cheese sandwich.

There's a dead body facedown in the toilet. A large burlap sack shoots up from the tub, muffled screams seep out as the sack shifts wildly. Chats doesn't blink, doesn't even bother setting down his sandwich. He whips out a tactical knife and rips a single slice, cutting through the sack and the throat of the poor bastard inside with razor precision. The sack drops back down into the tub with a thump, crimson pouring down the drain. Chats calmly nibbled his grilled cheese.

Rasnick takes a big snort, taking down the last line of coke with authority. "The last asshole? Waingrow? No idea what the hell he's sending out."

9

A lump of a security guard sits at a desk across the sprawling marble lobby of a nondescript office building. His post, his place in life as it were, rests among this vast tomb of a space. It's the kind of building you'd hate to work in, but have to.

The burned-out shell of a man nurses a cup of the building's complementary, horrible, coffee. Starbucks? Coffee Bean? Those are a fantasy on his salary. Hell, it's not even fucking Folgers.

He wears a fading gold nametag which reads LEON.

It sags crooked on his semi-pressed uniform. No gun, but he does have a belt with a walkie and a stick. Leon figures if something should actually happen he could use the stick to tap S.O.S into the walkie as he waits to bleed out from the bullet wounds. All this *gear* is designed to give the illusion of safety, the appearance of actual police; it's not fooling anyone.

Dressed in his grey, unflattering guard garb, Leon stares out into the empty office floor. He's barely hanging onto the handsome he once had, his once Greek God body now a shadow of its former glory. He can still gut through a mile run, maybe, but he's not going to pass any tests at Quantico. Leon has seen some tough days since Mexico. He spins his wedding ring on the desk, eyes drifting back and forth from the hypnotic spinning ring to a slow-as-hell clock on the wall.

When is this shit over?

A janitor buffs the floor, adding a layer of white noise to the deafening silence. He glances over to Leon, feels for the man. Leon sits there night after night sucking down bad coffee, never saying more than four or five words. The janitor forces eye contact with an exaggerated wave. "Later, Leon. You be well."

Leon slaps his hand down, stopping the spinning wedding ring cold. "Yeah."

At the employee lockers just off the lower level parking garage, Leon changes from his guard duds into street wear. These clothes aren't much better: tube socks, bad jeans, bad flannel…bad look overall.

He grabs his thermos.

Takes a squirt.

Clocks out.

As part of his nightly routine, he hits a bar on Wilshire not far from the building. At least it's his routine when he works. On his nights off he rarely gets out of bed. Leon sits alone at the bar, whiskey shots five deep with a Bud chaser close behind. LA's elite passes around him as if he was a pothole. The cocaine and boob job crowd have better things to do than pay attention to a guy they write off as some homeless dude at the bar.

Leon drains his shots one by one. It's an assembly line process that he's worked out—the assembly line of a fully functional alcoholic. He makes a face, upset that his head is still racing. The booze is supposed to at least slow that down. It doesn't, and that pisses Leon off. The booze actually cranks up his thoughts, hands them a microphone, and shoves them into the spotlight. That myth he heard about drinking to forget? Utter shit.

Leon remembers everything. He can even recall a time in his life when he really didn't drink at all. Wasn't so long ago. He used to have a nice home with a great Labrador, surrounded by nice crap from Pottery Barn. He used to have a kind, beautiful wife. There were friends and cookouts and football parties and talk about having children. His head keeps spinning back to the kind, beautiful wife, back to his is time with her. Remembers the laughter and smiles, the time when he didn't hate everyone and everything.

Not like now.

Now? Life consists of work, drinking, *Seinfeld* and *Family Guy* reruns, then some quick masturbation to free porn clips online before passing out. He doesn't speak to anyone he doesn't have to. Even prefers the drive-thru to communicating face-to-face at a counter. Orders things online when he can. Leon's built a life that is contained, controlled and void of emotional interaction of any kind. It's how he wants it.

He wanted that other life gone. Eased. Stuffed in a furnace and set ablaze. Wanted that house, the Lab and the wife to go away. And fuck you, Pottery Barn. He pushed it all away after Mexico. After Big Ugly took him captive.

Those days, weeks and months with that man have all bled together in Leon's head. Time meant nothing after awhile. Leon doesn't remember everything, which is probably best. He remembers flashes of dark places, moments of terror, sudden violence then days of nothing but breathing.

Oh yeah, there was humiliation too.

Then, completely out of nowhere, there would be a random day where a steak dinner would appear, served by a gorgeous blonde offering body massages and sex. Leon took the steak, but thanked the blonde for the offer and declined the sex. Sometimes Big Ugly would read Leon poetry. Or children's books, Or pull Leon's eyelids open forcing him to watch *The Sound of Music* spliced together with German snuff films.

On the last day, Big Ugly announced he was bored with Leon.

He calmly stated they were going to fight to the death. Leon's mind was gone by then, but somehow he understood. He even thanked Big Ugly for the opportunity. Leon was brought to a room, a very nice room that had crystal chandeliers…and a cage filled with medieval weapons. It was a real gladiator style affair, complete with an audience of half-naked women and men in suits. After what Leon had been through, none of this seemed strange at all. Almost expected, actually.

It took a few minutes for Leon's eyes to adjust after being in the dark during all the days prior. It's mostly a blur, but Leon does clearly recall Big Ugly coming at him with an axe to start. There were punches thrown, along with near misses from weapon strikes. It was a brutal struggle that seemed to last for hours.

Then there was a moment that changed everything.

A tiny sliver of time where luck and skill came together. Leon landed a punch that caught Big Ugly completely off guard. It was nothing special, not some special martial arts kick or a devastating combination drawn from Krav Maga. Just a wildly thrown haymaker that happened to catch Big Ugly just right; a fist that crash-landed to the temple and knocked Big Ugly out cold.

The audience went silent when Big Ugly dropped like a sack of meat. They all stopped breathing. Their master was down for the count.

That didn't happen. Big Ugly didn't lose.

Leon gathered himself and dragged his battered remains to the door of the cage. A group of the suits quickly beat him unconscious, of course, but later Leon woke up on a beach in Santa Monica. He couldn't believe it.

He was free, sort of.

Leon returned to the FBI and his wife. He tried to get back to his old life, tried hard to fall back into routines, but it wasn't easy. He was a P.O.W returning home, and everyone knew it was going to take time. There were medical and physiological evaluations, and lots of counseling. But life was slowly beginning to take shape again…until that video went viral.

Big Ugly released highlights of Leon's captivity. Moments that Leon didn't even remember, locked away out of self-defense. Now they were posted online, and subsequently emailed to the FBI, Leon's family, friends, and a special private message sent to his wife. What was on that video could not be unseen, could never be forgotten. No one ever talked directly to Leon about what was on the video, and Leon decided to never watch it. The expressions on their faces and the tone of their voices told Leon all he wanted to know. He heard the snickers in the hallways, the hushed tones that would go silent just as he entered a room. Ultimately it was the look in his wife's eyes. She tried to hide it, but it was there.

He started to resent others for not living through what he had, began to hate them for not being him.

He hated himself.

Everyone told Leon it was okay, but he knew it wasn't. He retreated deep inside himself, put himself into his own private exile. He pushed everything and everyone away. Knowing that his time with Big Ugly changed him forever and there was no going back, Leon left the FBI, his wife and his life. Hopefully his wife would find someone else who loved her, someone who wasn't broken and could never be put back together again. Someone who'd love her enough to let her go if that's what it took… like Leon did.

All of this passes through Leon's mind each night as he relentlessly pounds booze, and every night it doesn't get any easier.

He takes another shot, chases it, then slams another even faster. Leon's machine is working overtime, but his little pity party routine is stopped dead in its tracks by a voice behind him.

"Leon?"

10

A mushroom cloud blooms behind Leon's eyes as Cooper takes a seat next to him, motioning to the bartender for another round. He looks to Leon with great sympathy. "Sorry doesn't seem to quite cut it…"

Smash.

Leon shatters his bottle of Bud on Cooper's head, exploding from the bar stool and ramming Cooper into the wall. "What the fuck man?" yells the bartender. Cooper pulls his badge and calls out so everyone can hear him clearly. "FBI. Please give us the room." No one moves.

"Now!"

The bartender and the few remaining tipsy stragglers stumble to the exit. Leon is on fire. His eyes bulge. He can taste strangling the life from of this man and decides to give it a shot. "You left me to die in Mexico."

Cooper fights for air. "I'm here to make it right."

"Make it right? Look at me. I'm leftover scraps, a fraction of a fraction. Make it fucking right?" Leon lets him go and takes a seat—goes back to his booze. "What do you want, Cooper?"

Cooper puts pressure on his bleeding head. "I have an offer."

Leon throws back a final drink then heads for the door. "I'll counter with fuck your mother."

"There's been a Big Ugly sighting."

Cooper's words stop Leon dead in his tracks. He can't help but think of the implications of Cooper's statement. Cooper knows he has his full attention as he continues. "Doren and the other heads of state are putting together some fellowship of psychos to go after him. I can get you in."

"To do what?" asks Leon.

"Kill Big Ugly."

Leon turns to face Cooper.

"I'm offering you a chance for the big payback. A chance to silence all that shit rattling around your head," says Cooper. He shifts his tone, uncomfortable to even talk about it. "I know what he did you to."

Leon explodes, "You know shit!"

"I know you escaped within an inch of your life. I know you got laughed out of the FBI. I know you swept your wife from your life. And I know Big Ugly's been a big fuckin' pain in your ass." Cooper sucks in through his teeth. "Sorry, wrong thing to say."

Leon fires *eat shit* eyes at Cooper—that last statement was unnecessary, a cheap shot. He resets, explains as if to a child. "I escaped, and there's a lot I don't remember."

Cooper lets it go. "Look, I can give him to you. I can serve him up real special, but there's something you need to do for me."

Getting Ugly

"Takes some serious balls to show up looking for a favor. I lost everything. I got within a foot of that monster, and you served *me* up real special to *him*."

"Everybody was ordered off of him, even though we had an ocean of evidence. They destroyed his files, closed all open cases and investigations against him. They wiped him off the books, off the grid…off the earth."

"Why?" Leon asks.

"Big Ugly took out a den of high-end call girls before he disappeared. Killed the madam, shot the girls, then tore the place apart. Back at the Bureau there's a belief, one I happen to share, that Big Ugly found something, dirt on people who don't like to be dirty. Senators, Supreme Court justices. Don't know what he's got for sure. Could be video, audio, accounting records. Nobody's talking, but whatever it is, it's made Big Ugly untouchable. That's why you were left twisting in Mexico."

Leon slides back onto his stool, reaches across and pulls a Wild Turkey bottle from the other side of the bar. Taking it up a notch.

Cooper knows he has to get to the point, fast. "I can't send anybody else. Any involvement by me or the Bureau and word will spread. You're not FBI, you're not on anybody's radar. There are no eyes on you. Technically, this conversation isn't happening. But I'll set you up right; I got a big fucking bag of guns out in the car."

Leon takes a pull straight from the bottle. Cooper drags up a stool next to him. "I can't do a thing about the wife, but I can get your pension back. Get ya back your badge, maybe some of your pride and a bit of your soul. But that's if, and only if, you can get whatever Big Ugly has. We can put away some serious assholes and do some real good, Leon." Cooper is getting to him. Leon takes another gulp. "You used to care about that kinda shit, Leon."

A slow burn snakes up Leon's spine.

He lowers the Wild Turkey from his lips.

"You had me at kill Big Ugly."

11

Brobee, Rasnick, Oleg and Vig stand waiting next to a small hanger which houses a Gulfstream G280. Brobee is not happy. "The fuck is everybody?"

Rasnick, annoyed beyond reason, is forced to suffer this fool. "They'll be here."

Brobee bites a nail. "Fuckin' hungry."

"Stop talking," Rasnick snaps.

"A bit parched too…"

Brobee's bitching is stopped short as he's distracted by the sight of Pike and Patience strutting in. Pike is shirtless, a black blazer barely covering his two shoulder holsters. Patience's sundress clings to her sultry body. She loosely holds a Beretta in hand, a submachine gun slung around a shoulder. A Rambo worthy strap of clips parts her breasts. A little extra accessory, just to make sure you notice them.

Brobee notices. He stares, bug-eyed. "I just might love her."

Pike and Patience take positions in front of the group. They speak over each other, completing the sentence started by the other. Not in a rude way, or that *I know this person so well, married 20 years* kind of way. Their speech reflects the deep bond between them. It's a reckless, bottomless well that borders on—well, not borders...it is—violent obsession.

Pike announces, "Pike and Patience, ready to..."

"Make a buck and..." Patience continues.

"Kill a fuck," Pike finishes.

Rasnick's eyes roll. *Are you kidding me?*

Pike and Patience lock into a deep, tongue-wrapped kiss. It's nice for them, but dammed uncomfortable for everybody else. Brobee stutters, "Ahhh, I gotta frisk ya." He moves toward Patience, trying to figure out how to touch her in a way that won't repulse her, too much, and still work in his needs. Pike slaps him with a firm, open hand. At least he spared Brobee the embarrassment.

Next to join the party is Chats. It's as if ice could walk. Everybody immediately tightens up, not even really knowing why. They are all armed and have been in some pretty ugly spots, but when this guys walks in—*shit*. Chats walks past them without even a hint of eye contact and boards the plane without ceremony.

Pike looks to Brobee. "Gonna frisk him, ya fuckin' freak?"

"I'll...maybe later." Brobee motions to Pike. "Come on, tough guy. Open the jacket. Arms up." Pike humors the little guy and allows Brobee to pat him down.

Leon hovers outside the hangar watching it all. He can't believe he's here. *What the hell am I doing?* He pulls a flask and fires down a swig. He lets the whiskey burn down his chest, knowing he has to do this, has to go in there and do this thing. This is a once in a lifetime opportunity, the kind of second chance most people will never get. It's what people fantasize about after someone does something shitty to them. *If I'd only done X or said Y to that asshole.* Most fantasy do-over's don't contain the levels of violence and human suffering as Leon's case, but it's all relative. Leon takes another swig, swishes it around his mouth and makes his move inside.

Everyone gives Leon a look as he walks in. The group of killers lay hard eyes on him with blank expressions, giving Leon nothing in the way of greeting. None of them recognize him. Leon takes in their stares. *Nothing new,* he thinks. *Just tough guys being tough.*

Patience looks him up and down, perhaps a bit too long for Pike's taste. Brobee pats down Pike, finds a cell. Drops it in a bag and says, "Nobody's calling anybody, nobody's tracking us anywhere."

"Why's that, Sports Fan?" Pike asks.

"You motherfuckers are on a need-to-fucking-know basis, and you don't need to fucking know where the fuck we're going. I know how this movie ends—I tell you how to get to Big Ugly, you don't need Brobee anymore, you shoot Brobee. Not today, bitches."

Rasnick tries not to smirk.

Brobee tries not to drool over Patience. "You're next, beautiful." Patience is all too aware of her gifts and their ability to crush the superficial male. Her words glide from her tongue. "Be gentle." She lets her guns and ammo drop…then her sundress.

Patience is a jaw-dropping display of a woman. A Victoria's Secret model, criminally insane edition. Brobee doesn't know what to do.

She locks eyes on Leon. "See anything?"

Pike can't take it. He slaps Patience with a hard backhand. Everybody goes silent. Patience touches her lip with hurt in her eyes, but she's no garden-variety abused spouse. She puts a foot to Pike's balls, releases a war cry and pounces with reckless abandon. The lovers punch, spit and claw at each other. Rasnick motions to Vig and Oleg to break it up. They pull the two off each other, Patience's feet still flying as she's dragged away from Pike.

Patience and Pike catch their breath, then shove Vig and Oleg aside. They rush to each other, colliding in an anger-soaked kiss. Hands groping. Moans vibrating. Bloody lips pressed hard together. The others share a look between them.

That's fucked up.

The ragtag crew cruises through the clouds toward their mission of murder, surrounded by the Gulfstream's plush leather and luxury.

Leon keeps an eye on everything and everyone, sizing them up one by one. Breaking up his analysis is a constant, dull, thumping coming from the bathroom. Pike and Patience are joining the mile high club. Muffled, awkward grunts and moans seep out from the lavatory, along with bits of dirty talk.

"Spit in my mouth," barks Pike.

Leon shifts uncomfortably in his seat. Rasnick looks at the ceiling. Vig and Oleg share a vodka bottle. Chats locks an icy stare out into nothing while he cleans his teeth with a tactical knife.

Brobee eyes Leon. "I know you." Leon turns to find Brobee about two inches from his face.

"No, you don't."

"Yeah, yeah I do. Where do I fucking know you?" Brobee asks.

The pleasure moans and thumps from the bathroom get louder, now sounding like rabid monkeys trapped in a box.

Brobee doesn't let it go with Leon. "You been on TV?"

"No."

"Prison?"

"No."

"Punch my nipple," orders Patience.

Vig leans over, offering Leon a hit from his bottle. Leon declines. Vig insists. "Drink."

Leon tries being polite. "I'm good."

Rasnick joins the conversation. "You should take that drink."

"You my sponsor?" asks Leon.

"You a gay?" asks Oleg.

Vig pushes the bottle at him again. "Drink it."

Leon works to remain cool. "I'd rather keep a clear head before this…exercise."

Rasnick says, "Sauce helps Vig and Oleg. Frees the mind."

"The soul," add Vig and Oleg in harmony.

"And the soul," grins Rasnick.

Leon flashes a blank stare. "Congratulations." A knife flies, sticking with a thunk about an inch from Leon's face. He whips around to see Chats staring. "What the fuck, man?"

Rasnick puts a hand on Leon. "Chats doesn't talk. That's his way of asking, 'What's your fucking problem, fucko?' His words, not mine."

"Ever consider sign language?" Leon asks. Chats shakes his head. *Nope.*

A Comanche war cry booms from the bathroom as Pike's climax rattles the cabin. A moment of silence, then Pike exits. "Now I can get my murder on." Patience slips out adjusting her dress, flicks something from her finger. She notices the eyes on Leon, the tension in the cabin. She lets the words slip out like releasing a pressure valve. "What's up boys?"

Rasnick turns back to Leon. "Who are you, dude?"

Pike joins in. "Yeah, chief. I know these other bitches from around the way. Work acquaintances and so on…" Pike's words are cut short by Patience sliding in with sleepy, bedroom eyes on Leon. She wipes the corner of her mouth with the back of her hand then addresses Leon. "Who the hell are you?"

Tension picks up a notch.

People start fingering weapons.

Brobee addresses the cabin. "Easy, you animals. I've seen this guy somewhere, just can't place him."

Leon takes a breath. He really thought this wouldn't come up, but realizes now there is no way to ignore the situation. He clears his throat. "Waingrow asked me to come as a favor to him. I know Big Ugly. Been tracking him for years. Came close in Mexico, but he got the jump on me."

"But you're alive," states Rasnick, a note of disbelief in his voice.

"Yeah, this motherfucker, this Big Ugly?" Pike says. "From what I hear, live and let live ain't his way."

Leon tries to deflect the subject. "It's not important. What is important is we need to…"

"Fairly important, I think," says Pateince.

Pike wraps an arm around her waist. "Yup."

"I agree," Rasnick adds. "I mean, we need to know everything about our team and our target, right?" Chats flips his knife with a nod. Leon takes a beat trying to sort through his words. "He wanted to make an example of me, send a message. So he set me free."

Brobee heads snaps up. A light bulb goes off, then shatters. He can barely contain himself, fumbling to get the words out as fast as he can. "Holy fucking shit! I remember. Ah man, it's you! I'm fucking sorry, man. Oh my God."

"What?" asks Rasnick.

"Nothing. He's got the wrong guy," says Leon.

"No, no I do not," Brobee continues. "Big Ugly and this poor bastard…there was video online."

Eyes around the cabin go wide, even Chats. Leon's lip trembles ever so slightly as he speaks. "I escaped, and that's it."

Brobee keeps riding his train of thought. "Fucking awful, horrific. Bad, bad, bad."

Pike just wants to know. "What happened?" Brobee leans in and whispers into Pike's ear. Pike makes a face like he swallowed a bug wrapped in dog shit. Can't even look at Leon, all he can do is glance to his shoes.

Leon spits out, "Nothing happened. I busted out and escaped. Nothing happened."

Patience is almost bouncing out of her seat wanting to know. Pike whispers in her ear and her gorgeous features melt into a response similar to Pike's. She looks to Brobee in disbelief.

Brobee says, "It was all over the web. There was this comment forum; it was big deal."

Leon's anger ripples just below his skin. "I said nothing happened." He stops as he watches the whisper-wave spreads the story through the cabin and the remaining members of the crew.

Brobee asks, "Somebody got a laptop? I'll pull it up"

Leon loses it. Cover be damned. "Nothing fucking happened, you fucking retarded cocksuckers! Now shut the fuck up before I execute every fucking last one of you."

The cabin goes silent.

Really, what do you say?

Leon takes a shaky breath, pulling it together best he can. "Do you people have any idea who we are going after? This guy will burn down your dreams and eat your soul. If he likes you, he'll *just* kill you." Silence as the crew shares looks. "He is absent conscience, heart, or any form of reason. Living, breathing evil with 2400 SAT score. Do not, please, do not take him lightly or we will all die, badly."

The crew takes a moment to soak in Leon's words, his sincerity. It's all over him; he has seen things that no man should see.

Slowly the cabin begins to swell with laughter. The crew can't contain themselves. Patience is close to rolling in the isle. Chat snorts.

Pike busts out, "It was on the web?"

"Oh yeah, man, it was epic," wails Brobee.

A good time, all at Leon's expense.

12

In the hall in front of the penthouse suite, the same penthouse where the crime lords met, two armed goons guard the door, another at the elevator. The elevator doors open, and as the goon on elevator duty turns he catches a silenced 9mm to the head.

Goon one down.

Buster and Talley spring from the elevator wearing ski masks, black painter coveralls zipped to the neck, shoes covered. Buster blasts out the camera overhead while Talley takes out the two remaining goons at the door with head shots. The whole thing takes four seconds, maybe. Impressive, to say the least.

Inside the penthouse stand more goons, shoulder holsters heavy with guns at the ready. Cherrito and Waingrow are watching a Lakers game. Bosko sits in a chair reading *People*. Doren is resting comfortably in another room.

The room's door lock clicks, light going green. The door flies open as the masked Buster and Talley storm in. Their movement is constant, efficient, with not a single motion or bullet wasted. Controlled three round bursts. These are not meth-zombies shooting up a trailer park in search of a hundred bucks and a roll of quarters. These are highly trained individuals who do this kind of thing for a paycheck, pension and dental. The goons are dead before they can even draw their weapons, let alone fire a shot.

Cherrito and Waingrow are next.

They are unceremoniously removed from this Earth with a shots between the eyes. Bosko barely looks from his magazine, a crime lord thinking he's untouchable, that nobody would have the sack to even think about doing what they are doing. Bosko mutters, "Cocksucking..." before being silenced by Buster's bullet between the eyes. A plum of blood pops as Bosko's body is blown back over his chair.

Buster and Talley scan the room for Doren. The cowboys from hell slip into a side bedroom, where they find Doren sitting up in bed, enjoying soup. Doren looks them over, acknowledges his fate. He knew this day would come. Rarely do people like Doren die naturally. He says, "Just do it."

Done.

Buster and Talley remove their masks, quickly moving back to the living room. They tear away their coveralls, revealing blazers and slacks that look a lot like private security garb. Much like the uniforms the dead goons in the hallway were wearing, actually. They exit into the hallway, where they stand on either side of the penthouse doors with 9mms drawn as if they are about to go into the room for the first time. They wait. Buster rolls his eyes, impatient as hell. Talley knows his brother and instructs him, "Wait for it." Buster's eyes dance, his impulsive streak running wild as he spits out, "Fucking useless security shit stains."

"Shut. The. Fuck. Up."

"You shut up."

Elevator dings.

Buster and Talley get into character, snapping on the looks of panicked, dumbfounded, dipshit security guards. They start with the heavy breathing and plant looks of fear and concern on their faces. A team of security guards pours out of the elevator with guns drawn. Everything about them is identical to Buster and Talley. The lead guard slips up next to them, looks them over. He doesn't recognize them, but they are wearing the correct uniform and a good supervisor tries to avoid looking like an idiot at all costs. "What happened?"

The two brothers give the performance of a lifetime. Talley pants like a mutt, fakes terror and stutters while saying, "I think…I think…they're still in there, sir." Buster squeaks out, "They're armed, sir." The lead guard puts a calming hand on Buster's shoulder. Buster looks into his eyes and nods. *I'll be strong for you sir.* The lead guard motions for the rest of the team to move in around the door. As they do, Buster and Talley slip back toward the elevator. The lead guard address whoever he thinks is in the room in his best movie badass voice. "Okay, let's not get anybody hurt."

The elevator door closes.

Buster and Talley are gone baby gone. In the elevator, Buster giggles. *That was enjoyable.* Talley pulls out the GPS monitor that's tracking their brother, Rasnick.

"Where the fuck are they?" asks Buster.

Talley scrunches his nose. "They keep going in circles. It's like they're…"

13

"Lost?"

Rasnick stares out in the wilderness. "Fucking lost? You have no clue where we are?"

The bus of an SUV cruises down a one-lane road that snakes through a seemingly endless patch of dense woods. The crew fills the three rows of Chevy seating, Patience nestled in Pike's lap. A lot of pissed off looks fire in Brobee's direction, and he tries to hide the truth as he rides shotgun, Rasnick at the wheel.

"I'm not lost."

"Really? Fantastic. Where are we?" snaps Rasnick.

"We're close."

"Bullshit," snorts Vig. On cue Oleg chimes in, "Fucking bullshit, man."

Brobee can't believe this; he knows what he saw dammit. "It was dark as shit that night. Take it easy, you animals, I'll find it."

Pike fidgets, annoyed. This makes Patience annoyed. She barks, "This is a joke, right?" Leon keeps to himself, but his face says it all. *Fuck me.* His mind even drifts to a place that thinks his office building security gig maybe wasn't all that bad.

Brobee is completely flustered. "Look, goddammit, I trying here. I'm trying, damn, ok?"

Chats jams a knife into the headrest next to his ear. Leon looks to Chats then taps Brobee. "Think he's saying trying is for pussies." Leon leans into Chats. "Close?" Chats nods.

Brobee's eyes lock.

Just over the hill.

In the distance, shining like a diamond in a goat's ass.

Brobee yelps, "There!" His stolen Caddie sits on the side of the road like a hooker's corpse, right where he left it. "Stop!"

The Suburban's brakes lock.

The crew moves through the same woods Brobee braved less than 48 hours ago. A heavily armed band of the most ill-tempered, badass Cub Scouts ever known, Brobee leads the way, still not completely confident where he's going. They've been trudging through these woods for a while and the natives are getting restless, again.

Pike looks up, down, all around the suffocating woods. "He build a nest or some shit?", "You'll see, fuck face," spits Brobee.

"Been staring at trees for two hours now," says Patience.

"We're good. Trust. Please?" begs Brobee.

Rasnick and Leon are bringing up the rear, staying a few steps behind the rest of the pack. Rasnick turns to Leon. "You said you tracked Big Ugly for a time, right?" Leon nods, not sure where this is going. "Who is he?" Rasnick asks. Leon fights off a grin. "Nobody knows for sure. Some think he was a Marine once, maybe CIA. Maybe trained in Asia. Contract killer for a time. Some even believe he was a cop for awhile."

"About to be a broke, dead bitch," interrupts Pike.

"Absolutely," purrs Patience.

Leon hopes they're right.

Pike keeps spewing testosterone. "Don't know everything, but I know my skills, and they are sharp, tight and ready to light some fire on his ass." Patience throws an arm around him and Pike spanks her backside. Leon thinks about using a nail and hammer to keep his eyes from rolling. Instead he says, "Confidence is cute, but a healthy dose of fear might keep you alive."

Patience stops cold, stares at Leon as if he slapped her Mama. "Fear? You be afraid, pillow bitter." That earns a laugh from the rest of the crew.

Leon looks to Rasnick. *Be afraid*.

Rasnick gets it.

The crew stops under a massive tree, its roots spiraling out of the ground and back in like a ride at a water park. They've reached a bullet-riddled body slumped against the tree's trunk. Brobee recognizes the face. "Ahhh, man."

"You knew him?" asks Rasnick.

"I—yeah, I stole his truck when I left. Feel bad, a little responsible."

Leon looks on. *A little? These people are unbelievable.*

Rasnick motions for them to keep moving and they continue their march through the thick woods. Something bothers Leon, a question he needs answered. "Hey, Brobee."

"Yo."

"Did he see you?"

"Who?"

"Santa. Who do you think? Big Ugly, asshole."

"No, no way."

Leon's face tightens. "You sure about that?"

Rasnick joins in. "If we're walking into a goddamn slaughter, so fucking help me." Brobee attempts to reassure them. "I'm damn positive, man. C'mon." Everybody stops. All eyes bore through Brobee. He can't believe the lack of trust from his brothers and sisters in arms. "He did not fucking see me."

He's sure.

Really sure.

So sure.

Kinda sure.

PART III
some kinda Willy Wonka prick cocksucker.

14

Less than 48 hours ago…

Brobee stood at the edge of the clearing, mouth and eyes agape.

Up ahead was the object of his horror.

Up ahead…

Big Ugly.

Forty-something, dressed in a slick, tailored Fioravanti suit and, oddly enough, not ugly at all. Actually better looking than probably 99% of men walking the earth. Cigar in his mouth, scotch in hand, and his baby blues locked on Brobee from across the yard. Big Ugly flashed a chilling smile, took a beat, then gave a tiny finger wave to Brobee.

Piss flowed.

Brobee bolted.

Big Ugly stood in front of a 28,000 square foot sprawling mega mansion. *His* mansion. Aside from the open land that immediately encircles the home, the area is completely surrounded, protected by the dense trees and wilderness. This place won't show up on any map. A stable of cows sits to the side of the jaw-dropping home. There is no visible road that leads in or out of Big Ugly's land.

This is a lap of luxury that does not want to be found.

Big Ugly's right-hand man, Bobby, runs from the house. Big Ugly's gaze is still fixed out into the distance as Bobby races up to him. He's knee-deep in a thinking man's trance. Bobby controls his breath. "Big Ugly, I saw something breached the red line." Big Ugly doesn't bother with eye contact as he cuts Bobby off. "Somebody. Somebody breached, Bobby.

"I'll get the dogs." Bobby pulls an old school Uzi while springing into Code Blue mode.

"No, Bobby. Not this time."

Bobby stops. "Did they see you?"

Big Ugly cracks a grin. "Oh, yes. Saw me…knows me."

"Interpol? CIA?"

"No."

"How did he find you?"

Big Ugly puffs his cigar. "Luck. Fate. Doesn't really matter."

"I need to get you out of here. They'll send people."

Big Ugly finally turns to Bobby. "Oh, people will come, Bobby. Nasty, filthy, scary people. People with bad childhoods and questionable morals will descend on me with guns, bloodlust, and visions of murderous mayhem dancing in their heads. But Bobby, make no mistake…" Big Ugly puts the cigar out in his own palm with a sizzle. "I'm not fuckin' going anywhere."

Inside the mega mansion Big Ugly glides through a foyer that rivals the lobby of Caesars Palace. Bobby stays close, trying to reason with the unreasonable. "I know you haven't been yourself recently." Big Ugly appreciates the concern—not really. Bobby continues, "Depression is a natural response…"

Big Ugly spins, jamming his Smith & Wesson down Bobby's throat. "Depression is for cock deprived housewives. Do you find me cock deprived?"

Bobby gurgles a "No."

"I've walked on water, turned water into scotch. I've cleaned out the Gods—stuffed their balls in my pocket and then simply walked away. You know the win/loss record for people who nail the big score and then retire to the sweet life?" Bobby shakes his head. Big Ugly completes his sermon. "There's one winner and two million, six hundred and fifty eight thousand limp-dick losers. And Bobby-Boy, I'm the one."

Big Ugly slips his gun from Bobby's lips. "Warriors are born to war, not to hide. Sure, I've done the cocaine and orgy thing for good while…"

Bobby wants to appear agreeable. "And done it well."

Big Ugly chews on that a bit. "I have, haven't I? I need to…need something. Killing the occasional hiker ain't cutting it anymore. Oh yeah, there's a guy out on the road who just lost his truck. Would you kill him and leave him in the woods for me?"

Bobby doesn't bother answering. He knows it's neither needed or appreciated. Big Ugly pauses, wants to frame this the proper way. "I'm bored, man."

Bobby looks into his master's crestfallen eyes. Bobby even feels sorry for him. "I understand, but are you sure?"

"I fucked a goat yesterday, Bobby. A goat."

Bobby can only stare back. Really, there's not much to say to that.

Getting Ugly

Big Ugly spins a finger in the air, a signal for Bobby to round up the staff.

Big Ugly and Bobby enter an oversize formal dining room. This is where royalty grazes. Standing in a long line at full attention are maids, butlers, kitchen help and a scholarly-looking man. He wears a lab coat and a stethoscope. Not because he really has to, but because Big Ugly has him on staff to be a doctor and, by God, in Big Ugly's mind he should look like a doctor.

Big Ugly walks down the line, Bobby next to him carrying a basket filled with stacks of rubber band bound cash. As Big Ugly shakes the hand of each staff member, he hands him or her a severance stack.

Big Ugly reaches an attractive maid and gives her a nipple twist. She smiles. She gets an extra stack. He reaches the doctor.

"I'm not leaving you here," announces the doctor.

Big Ugly nods.

"You need help. Treatments need to…"

Blam!

Big Ugly drops him with a bullet to the brain. The staff barely flinches; this happens somewhat frequently around here. Bobby motions to an open door leading to an adjacent room. The nondescript room contains a lone bed, a sand box, and walls padded with blue foam egg crates.

Brobee asks, "And them?"

Looking toward the room, Big Ugly eyes a row of five semi-nude hookers. "Get rid of them." Bobby moves towards them, not completely sure if he's supposed to kill them or just set them free. Big Ugly places a hand on Bobby. "On second thought, leave two."

The remaining staff and hookers exit with Bobby, who is carrying the dead doctor. They all pile into waiting Escalades. Bobby stuffs the doctor's body into the back of one Escalade and turns to his master with watery eyes. *Good-byes are hard.*

Big Ugly shows a flicker of humanity. "Bobby, words do not do justice." Bobby extends a hand. "It's been an honor and a privilege." Big Ugly hands him four stacks, pauses, then takes back one.

Bobby gets in and the Escalades drive off into the woods. Big Ugly watches them leave. He'll miss them, some of them.

Not really.

He snaps his fingers.

The Escalades explode, bursting into multiple fireballs.

Inside his home, Big Ugly stands in front of sound system that reaches from floor to ceiling. A hand carefully loads a CD. Yes, he still uses CDs. Can't very well have an iTunes account when you're trying to be a ghost, can you? The windows shake and the walls rattle as the rock anthem *For Those About to Rock (We Salute You)* booms. Big Ugly moves through the mansion with the music following him.

It's time to prepare for his guests.

Instruments of murder are laid out on an Olympic-size table, a white linen cloth underneath. Glocks, Colts, submachine guns, a sawed-off pistol-grip 12 gauge, an axe, a samurai sword, tactical knives, a whip, bullets and shells piled high. Weapons served up buffet style.

Big Ugly practices knife play in a mirror.

He tries out different gun at the in-house range, fine tuning his game.

Cleans each of his guns with the greatest of care, carefully inspecting every detail and then going over them again. He polishes a handcrafted samurai sword with a fine shammy.

Big Ugly sits naked in the middle of an indoor basketball court.

Old bullet wounds, knife scars, teeth marks decorate his chiseled body like medals of honor. With legs crossed, he lets his mind cleanse itself. Letting himself go, he releases his soul into deep mediation. The battle is won before it's fought. Big Ugly visualizes his war without knowing whom he will be fighting. It doesn't matter. They will die, and die badly. Big Ugly will be entertained. His mind weaves in and out of reality, and the false reality he's created over the years.

The lies, the covers, the truth…none of it is clear anymore. The stories he's used over the years range from him being an orphan to the son of a dentist, from an only child to the third child in a family of ten. He's been straight, homosexual, bi-sexual—there was also that thing with the goat, whatever that was. He's been married, divorced, murdered wives, strangled gay lovers and was the live-in penis for two bi Israel chicks for a bit.

He's deep down in his own head now.

The one thing, the only thing he wanted to hold onto, was his memory mother's face. No matter what happened, no matter how many false versions of him there were, he wanted to remember the face of his mother. The details of her life and the life Big Ugly had with her were not important—he sure as hell can't keep all that straight anymore—but if he could just hold onto Mom's beautiful face he could hang onto something that was still his own.

His mind fumbles through images of women he's known, fucked, killed, and seen on TV, but none of them are Mom. *Where is she? She's here somewhere, right?* He squeezes his eyes tight. Sweat trickles down his forehead as the faces spin faster and faster in his mind. *She's not there.* His brain is out of control, flipping through an endless loop, unable to find her.

Big Ugly pops his eyes open.

Snaps his fingers.

Fuck Mama.

Big Ugly surveys the impressive wardrobe in his gigantic walk-in closet. Silk button-downs, polished shoes, pristine suits hand-tailored by the finest craftsmen around the globe. He slips on a black Brioni suit that carries the price tag of a BMW. He tightens a blood red tie. He chooses socks with care. Shines a loafer.

All of this as if he was a knight selecting armor, suiting up in proper battle attire. Choosing the clothes he'd like to perhaps die in.

The room Big Ugly selected for his office is the size of the average tech start-up's entire building. It's filled with the best of everything, and when that best is outdated he gets the new best of everything.

Big Ugly takes a seat in front of a wall of monitors sporting a look that would make most GQ cover boys run away shrieking like frightened, homely bitches. He waits.

His eyes bounce off each screen, one after the other. He syncs a handheld, wireless LG video surveillance tablet. The touch screen now buzzes through the same views as the wall of monitors, missing nothing.

Touch of the screen…a bird flies.

Touch…Brobee's Cadi on the road, the crew's empty Suburban parked next to it.

Touch…a squirrel scampers.

Touch…big smile from Big Ugly. "Hola."

15

Out from the woods steps the crew, armed with enough firepower to invade a small country.

Brobee points to the mega mansion with great vindication and whisper-yells, "There. There, ya dicks. Everybody happy?"

Everyone soaks in the scope of the place.

Pike utters, "Ya fuckin' kidding me?"

"I pray the bastard did not spend all our money," says Vig.

"Pray the bastard is home," says Oleg.

Leon's focus is razor sharp as he takes note of everything. He feels it—something is off. "He knows we're here."

Rasnick studies Leon. "How do you know?"

In the distance there is the low hum of something coming their way. They turn to the hum, two four wheel ATVs motoring toward them. One ATV rides behind the other in a very careful, precise straight line. Manning the ATVs are two naked hookers, one blonde, one brunet. The male crewmembers' heads follow the dancing double Ds rolling their way. The off-road tires of the ATVs leave ruts in their wake.

Getting Ugly

Patience notices Pike taking in every not so subtle boob bounce and presses a .45 to Pike's head. Pike coughs, then recovers by quickly looking to his shoes. Chats scratches his nuts with a knife.

The ATVs come to a stop in front of the crew. The blonde hooker, the dumber of the two—cheerfully dumb, but dumb nonetheless—calls out like a medieval messenger. "I bring word from Big Ugly." She pauses to read her hand. "If you want blood, you got it."

Leon can't help but stare at the small black heart tattoo nestled just above her right breast.

The hookers blow the crew a kiss and ride off.

The crew looks to Brobee. He shrugs. "Perhaps he did see me." Brobee pulls a Glock while backing up toward the woods. "Well, kids, I'm outta here."

"No really, can't you stay?" Leon asks with fake sincerity.

Brobee keeps drifting backwards, making his getaway. "Cute. My role in this circle-jerk is done. Soooo, good luck with that Big Ugly thing. Looks hard…" A sudden crack from a high-powered rifle sounds, a bullet ripping Brobee's head off, ending his exit strategy. A heartbeat later his body flops to the grass.

The crew hits the dirt. Pike begins to shake, showing signs of his false bravado crumbling. He mutters, "Holy fuck—shit." Oleg jumps up, pulls his AK, and sprints toward the house.

Leon doesn't like the feel of this either. It's too… something. He calls out to Oleg, "Wait!" Oleg makes it maybe three steps before…

Boom!

A landmine sends Oleg's body flying. Earth scatters. Oleg's charred remains thump to the ground in three clumps of human-like pieces. A new level of fear has reached the crew.

Vig freezes at the sight his dead buddy.

Chats fires up a cigar.

Pike continues his shaking. Patience looks to her man, or what she thought was her man—this one has turned into a complete pansy.

Rasnick turns to the one person in the crew who seems to have a clue, Leon. "The fuck do we do now?" Leon has no real answer other than, "Try to stay alive." Patience is losing hers. "I'm gonna gut this piece of shit," she says to Pike. "Right, baby?"

Pike is jello.

Leon looks around, searching for inspiration. He spots the ruts left by the hookers' ATVs. He calls out the remaining members of the once proud crew. "There. Follow the tracks to the house."

Pike offers a counter strategy. "We could go back in the woods, regroup a bit?"

"Like Brobee?" asks Rasnick.

Leon keeps looking over the land, the situation, trusts his gut—he gets it now. He knows Big Ugly. As if thinking out loud he says, "He wants us to come inside."

Rasnick asks, "For what?"

Leon looks to the house. *Not sure yet.* He is sure that he has to either lead this pack of whackos into the house or sit there and die. Leon gets up, swallows hard, and starts walking along the tire ruts.

The rest of the crew shares a look. *Is he nuts?* Chats rises, then follows Leon. Rasnick is next. Patience motions for Pike to go. The man is a puddle. Patience punches him in the jaw with a crunch. Pike shakes his head. Patience jabs at him again, this time to the nose. Nothing. Patience stands up and attempts to stomps his balls. Pike finally snaps out of it, grabbing her foot and spinning her to the ground. He jams a Glock under Patience's chin. His breathing is hard, his eyes wild like a frightened animal. Patience smiles, getting to her feet. "There's my baby, come on now." She holds out a hand. Pike pulls it together, takes her hand, and the two follow Leon's lead.

The crew moves along the ruts with Vig bringing up the rear. He looks back to his fallen comrade Oleg and hate swells. Vig racks his AK. The crew is halfway between the woods and the Big Ugly's mansion. All is quiet for now, but their thoughts bounce, roll and catch fire knowing that anything could happen at any moment. Their breathing is accelerated, hearts racing, but down deep inside, each of them love this.

The crack of whip snaps in the distance. A voice booms with a cowboy yell. "Yeee-haaa!" The crew stops.

What.

The.

Hell?

A low rumble slowly rolls, quickly growing into rapid thumping. The ground shakes and trembles. Leon realizes what it is. *Shit!*

It's the heart-stopping sound of a stampede coming their way.

The herd of cattle runs riot from the stables in the distance, moving at amazing speed and kicking up earth in their path, storming headlong at Leon and company. This something not even Leon anticipated. Guns? *Sure*. Blood? *You bet*. Pain and anguish? *Without question*. But rumbling cattle driving at them with reckless abandon? No, that did not enter their minds.

Boom!

A cow goes flying as it hits a landmine. Beef sent flying end over end. Across the flood of livestock, a cow shoots up in the air every couple of seconds, with the shock and awe of the landmines causing the herd to stampede even harder towards the crew.

The crew is frozen by the remarkable sight. They can only look on. *Dear God!*

"Run!" screams Leon.

They sprint hard, legs pumping and knees riding high, all while trying to remain in the tire tracks. The rampaging cattle bear down on them like a bovine tsunami.

Boom!

Another cow is hurled airborne, flopping down within inches of Leon. He hurdles the meaty mess, landing in a pile at a side door to the mansion. He throws open the door and is immediately met by a shotgun blast. He manages to flip the door shut just in time. The door takes the shot, blasting it back open.

Leon tumbles back planting himself spread eagle against the wall, taking safety in the inches available to him as the stampede is almost there.

The remaining crew does the same, lining up as close to the wall as they can on the other side of the door. Everyone is as tight against the wall as humanly possible, all except for Vig.

Vig's grief-fueled rage gets the better of him when he sees Big Ugly through the blown out door. His veins pop. His mind unsnaps. Vig runs full tilt, crashing through what's left of the door while unloading his AK into the mansion. His wild bullets miss Big Ugly who, bored with this, calmly fires his sawed-off shotgun.

The scatter blast hits Vig, sending him flying backward just as the rambling stampede blows by, ripping Vig along with them. His body bounces along limply, contorting like a rag doll atop the raging grain-fed mass.

Along the wall the crew braces themselves as the rush of cattle rips past, trying to make themselves one with the bricks and mortar behind them. The cattle roar by, heading off into the woods. The crew gathers themselves. Leon moves closer to his side of the door as Rasnick does the same on the other side. They share a look.

A shotgun pump echoes from inside the house.

Leon pulls a tactical smoke grenade. Rasnick nods, turning to Pike, Patience and Chats huddled behind him. *Ready?* Leon tosses the grenade into the doorway. Smoke quickly spreads, overtaking the room and seeping back outside.

They hear a cough.

The crew all looks to Leon.

He gives the signal.

The crew unleashes a hellfire maelstrom of relentless fire, unloading buckets of bullets into the smoke. Leon empties his Glock, slam loads and waits. The others keep pounding away. Leon yells out, "Stop!" They don't. The bullets continue to run ripshit. Leon screams out again, nearly tearing a vocal cord. "Stop, dammit!" The rest of the crew finally ceases fire. They hold smoking guns at the ready.

The smoke starts to thin out.

All's quiet.

Leon slips inside the house, swinging his tricked out assault riffle from left to right. Checks the corners first, sweeping, clearing like a good boy should. Rasnick follows suit, sweeping the room like a pro, just like Leon. Leon takes note of Rasnick's technique.

The once Caesars Palace-like room is now a war-torn shit pile. Bullet holes decorate the walls, marble and granite gouged in chunks. Not a hint of Big Ugly. Pike, Patience and Chats file in with guns drawn.

Leon speaks low to Rasnick. "He's somewhere in the house."

"How do you know he didn't slip out the back?" asks Rasnick. "Maybe hauled ass to Switzerland or some shit?"

"Does it look like he's running scared?" asks Leon.

Chats pumps his shotgun, moseying up the spiral marble stairs toward a massive set of double doors. "Where are you going?" asks Leon. Nothing from Chats as he checks the knives that decorate his chest, then the 9mm at his side, before slipping through the doors. Patience agrees. "He's right. Divide and conquer." Pike finds his nuts again. "Hell yeah, baby doll." They start moving toward another set of doors on the right.

Leon grabs Pike's shoulder. "Let him go."

Pike whips his arm free. "He's gonna take all the money."

"Think. We're on his home field. This guy will chew us up one by one if we separate." Leon stops just short of adding *you fucking idiot* to the end of that sentence.

Pike fails to see the logic. "Fuck that. We split up and…"

"Dead this fool," Patience finishes.

Getting Ugly

Leon hates these people, he really does, but he realizes he needs them in order to survive this thing. He moves in front of Pike and Patience, working to maintain eye contact. Not unlike training animals, he realizes he needs to speak on their terms while maintaining some form of dominance. Leon says, "Our strength, our only strength, is we are four hard-hitting, ball-busting, badass fuckers here with some death to deal, and get paid doing it. Right?" It's a lot of work and hurts his head to talk this way, but Leon sees he's winning Pike and Patience over by spewing their special brand of bullshit. Leon now has their complete attention and keeps at it. "I need to know something. You got the heart for this?"

Rasnick watches, trying not to smirk. He does enjoy the show Leon is putting on.

"Let me think about it. How 'bout fuck you?" says Pike.

Patience nods, eating it all up with a spoon.

Leon smiles. "Good. Because you need to ask yourselves a serious question—are you here to cut the Devil's nuts off, or piss your panties?" Pike and Patience are all ears. Leon is feeling it now. He jerks his thumb. "Behind those doors is a nightmare greased for war." He turns an eye to Pike. "You go pussy on me, I'll fucking leave you dead on the floor."

Now all eyes are now on Pike.

He shrinks, knowing he can't really hide the way he reacted moments ago in the front yard. "I lost it a bit, okay? I'm better now." Leon raises an eyebrow. Patience knows Leon's concern is warranted—hell, she's concerned too—but Pike is her man, dammit. She blurts out, "He's fucking good, ok?"

Rasnick shifts, eyes the 9mm Berretta with the GPS grip that Talley gave him. He glances to the door, knowing his SWAT brothers are coming in at some point. Wishes they'd hurry the hell up.

Leon turns his attention to Rasnick. "And you?" Rasnick knows he needs to squash any doubters right here and now. He responds, "Don't waste my time. You? Questioning me? You fucking…"

"Then let's go," Leon says.

16

The Gentlemen's room.

This room is a finely woven mix of high-end strip joint and a Best Buy. Deep leather couches, plush chairs, massive screens everywhere showing various ESPN channels, along with three striper stages complete with polished brass poles. Colored lights twirl above the stages, with the rest of the room dimly lit. Along the far wall is a fully stocked bar that stretches up to a skylight in the ceiling. Rain starts to spatter on the windows, giving a new eerie feel to an already odd place. Nothing like walking through a madman's home equipped with in-house version of Scores.

Leon, Rasnick, Patience and Pike push through the doors, entering with caution. Rasnick and Leon sweep with trained efficiency, again checking corners and clearing the area.

Rasnick's method is perfect, and this isn't lost on Leon. "You ever in the military?"

Rasnick gives a defensive snarl. "Fuck no. Why?"

Patience jumps up on the center stage and begins working a striper pole. Pike loves it. Leon doesn't hate it, but feels the need to put this fire out before it gets out of control. "Really not the time." Patience fires off a sexual blast with a simple flicker of her eyes, a curl of her lip and an ever so slight hip roll. She works the pole like a pro, driving Pike crazy. He folds a dollar bill and bites down on it. Rasnick doesn't like them getting careless either. He ratchets up a harsh tone. "He's right, we need to move."

Patience slithers and slides, sexy pumping full stream. She crawls over to Pike, taking the dollar from his mouth with her teeth. They hold their stare. Leon thinks, *Don't do it on the stage, don't do it on the stage...*

A stream of gunfire cuts up the hardwood stage.

Pike rips Patience away. He comes up with a hand cannon in each fist, screaming and firing blindly at anything and everything. Patience follows suit laying down M4 submachine gun bursts. They fire in no particular direction, bullets searing air, rounds popping spastic. The bar shatters. Bottles pop. Booze rains. Sixty-inch screens get cut up to shit. Leon pushes over a table, taking cover with his tricked out AR-15 ready. Rasnick dives next to him. They scan the area.

There's nobody else in the room.

No Big Ugly.

"Stop!" yells Leon. Pike and Patience continue screaming and unloading bullets at nothing in particular. Leon gets to his feet. "Stop fucking shooting. Please!" Gunfire stops. *What the fuck?* glances all around. They all turn to Leon looking for something in the way of wisdom.

"He's not here. He's just fucking with us."

"How do you know?" asks Rasnick.

"Because we're all alive." Leon turns to Patience and Pike. "You wanna dance a little more, or can we get the fuck on with this?"

Getting Ugly

Leon leads with his AR, the rest following behind him with weapons tracking. They've entered a long corridor of a room that contains two-foot thick glass walls on either side. It's a room sized fish tank holding thousands of gallons of water and various aquatic life forms. What little light there is gives off a soft bluish glow to the room. Fish streak by the glass. Hundreds of them cut through the water surrounding the crew. It's as if SeaWorld had a Gun-Toting Wild Bunch Day. Pike taps the glass, pissing off the fish. Patience joins him. They stare childlike at the marine life, like two kids who've only seen fish on TV.

A large chunk of raw meat floats in the water. Leon takes note of a skeleton, stares hard. "Is that…a cow?"

Pike presses his nose to the glass.

A shark rips through the water inches from the Pike's face, jaws snapping taking the chunk of meat down whole. Pike almost shits himself. Pulls his guns, ready to blast away. Leon stops him. "Easy, Tex." Patience plays with Pike's hair, trying to sooth her boyfriend.

After Pike's blood pressure comes down to a manageable level he says, "This guy's some kinda Willy Wonka prick cocksucker."

Chats enters the Great Room, a room mammoth in scale with twenty foot high ceilings. The crystal chandeliers seem to float in air. Chats charges through; he couldn't care less about the décor or the fine craftsmanship or the time and effort required to put together a room like this. He moves with purpose, void of any skill or concern, without regard for clearing the room first for safety.

That shit's for Johnny Law.

Chats plows along like Michael Myers stalking a teenager, the big difference being that Chats doesn't give two shits about his prey's sex life and does not bother with a mask. He's extremely confident he'll kill whatever comes his way. He tries a set of doors. Locked. Pumps a round, blasts it open.

A sharp noise sounds from a stairway to the right.

Chats marches down a hallway to the set of stairs. Enters with sawed-off first. There's a heart-freezing stillness to the open space, only the rain from outside patters against the windows. This is the point when a weaker mind, a sane mind, would start to rethink strategy. Perhaps think of doing something other than driving into the heart of a certified killer's home. Others might even take this moment to analyze where they are in life, think about maybe making some changes. Chats does not take such a moment. Chats presses on with his hunt.

A platinum hatchet cuts through the air.

Chats pivots right, the hatchet thudding deep in the wall about a half-inch from his skull. All Chats sees is Big Ugly's shoe slipping through an exit. Chats unleashes a 12-guage fury while rushing the doorway. The door blows open, torn off its hinges from the pulverizing shotgun force.

Back in the Aquarium Hall, Leon, Rasnick, Pike, and Patience jump at the sound of the shotgun blasts. They rush to the doors.

Chats pushes through the doorway. No Big Ugly to be found. He's reached a locker room type shower area. Gold fixtures. Etched glass. Flat screens show a sharply edited montage of porn with fast cuts of gruesome Japanese horror movie death.

Something else catches Chats's attention. Up ahead, at the far end of the lockers stands Big Ugly.

Five Big Uglys, actually.

Multiple mirrors are angled perfectly to give five full-length reflections of Big Ugly in his exquisite suit…and the steel axe strapped to his back. Big Ugly gives him the finger—five actually.

Chats pumps and unloads, shattering the mirrors as if twenty disco balls exploded into a confetti shower. Chats shoves in fresh shells as the gentle tinkle of mirror bits fall.

A flat hand chops Chats in the throat as Big Ugly twists the shotgun loose from his grip, throwing it against the shower wall. Chats recovers with hard foot to Big Ugly's knee, putting him on the tile. Chats dives, wrapping his hands tight around Big Ugly's throat. Big Ugly counters by unsheathing the axe from his back, whipping it around like a windshield wiper.

Chats falls back, but not before the axe snips the tip of his nose. Blood spreads down his mouth and chin. Chats spits red, pulling his 9mm from his belt. Big Ugly springs like a cat from a bathtub, spinning, pivoting, and slipping away from the gun blasts into the next room, leaving Chats with nothing but the sound of empty shells bouncing off the tile. Chats can only grin as blood drips from his snipped nose.

Leon and the remaining crew rush down the hallway into the locker room.

Chats follows Big Ugly, entering mid-court onto a full-size basketball court marked with NBA specs, complete with a big-ass Jumbotron. On the other side of the court stands Big Ugly, who slips his axe behind his back and pulls his favorite Colt. Chats keeps his 9mm on Big Ugly, and the two hold guns on each other, taking a moment to size up their competition. Big Ugly takes a second to glance at the surveillance monitor app on his

Getting Ugly

tablet, where he sees Leon, Rasnick, Pike and Patience entering the shower room. With a flick of his thumb the Jumbotron lights up with a full image of Chats and Big Ugly on the court. He flicks his thumb again.

As Leon and company enter the shower room, a side door to another room swings open by itself. They glance at each other. *The fuck?* With guns raised they creep through the door, slipping into a room filled with rows of theater seating ten rows deep. But not your average bleacher seating. These are plush leather captain chairs with the initials BU embroidered on the backs.

The door slams behind them with a metal thunk.

The wall in front of them rolls down revealing a glassed-in view of the basketball court. Pike tries a door leading to the court. "Locked."

Rasnick pulls at the door they came through and it opens a bit. He keeps that info to himself. "Yeah, we're locked in."

Leon checks the glass. It's thick as hell, surely bulletproof.

All they can do is watch the two gladiators on the court. Sound is piped in through Bose speakers. On the basketball court is the show. The war. Guns on guns, psycho on psycho, Chats on Big Ugly.

Chats and Big Ugly lock eyes, grins spreading across their faces. Two warriors who know what is happening here—only one gets out alive. *It's cool.* They nod respectfully.

They go at each other in an all-out sprint. Both blasting, each weaving just enough for the bullets to whizz by. Chats dodges left, then right. Big Ugly spins and rolls, comes back up firing. The hardwood court is chewed up and spit out. They steamroll, bulls raging toward one another, getting closer and closer to impact,.

They collide at center court. Chats jams his 9mm to Big Ugly's temple, who swats it away as a bullet plows into center court. The battle, in all its glory, is mirrored up on the Jumbotron.

Big Ugly shoves his Colt into Chats heart. Chats grabs Big Ugly's wrist, twisting it away with a crack of ligaments. The Colt slides across the court, a stray bullet firing toward the glass viewing wall.

The bullet digs into the glass wall directly in front of Leon's face. He doesn't even blink as he watches on.

Chats and Big Ugly twist, tug, and pull as Big Ugly holds on to Chats's gun hand. Chats throws a head-butt into Big Ugly's face, which Big Ugly returns with an even harder forehead slam to what's left of Chats's nose. Chats stumbles back and Big Ugly rips the axe free, cutting off Chats's right hand in a single, clean swipe. The severed hand bounces to the hardwood, still gripping the 9mm.

Chats's body trembles. His eyes bulge, water, swell red. Yet, still not a single sound from the man as blood spits from his wrist stump. Big Ugly leaps, plunging his axe downward for the mother of all death chops. Chats rolls and the axe slams full force into the foul line, completely stuck in the wood.

Chats pulls a tactical knife from his ankle with his remaining hand. He flips the knife into an overhand grip. He swings and rips at Big Ugly with lightning fast, wind-cutting swipes, pushing Big Ugly away from the axe planted in the court. Big Ugly throws a quick jab, then lands a roundhouse. Chats takes the hits but keeps coming.

Getting Ugly

From the bleacher room the remaining crew watches on like they were at a UFC brawl. The hell-bent warriors on the court are getting closer and closer to the glass. Chats has his back to them. Big Ugly goes for a knockout uppercut. Chats pivots and comes up slicing Big Ugly's cheek.

Big Ugly takes a step back. Like Bruce Lee in *Enter the Dragon*, he touches his finger to his bleeding cheek, tastes it. Then, as if a switch was flipped, as if Big Ugly suddenly decided enough is enough, he grabs Chats's arm with amazing speed and force. The arm cracks, knife popping up, airborne. Big Ugly grabs another tactical knife from Chats's belt, then snatches the first blade in midair.

The crew is stone cold silent. Leon closes his eyes; he knows how this is going to end.

Holding the Ginsu-sharp tactical knives in each hand with an overhand grip, Big Ugly slices both hands in a scissor-whip across Chats's throat.

Chats's head slowly slides from his neck, landing with a single bounce. Blood pumps from the carotid arteries in the open neck. Big Ugly looks into the bleacher room at his captive audience. His stare is blank, calm, and chilling. He drops the knives, picks up his Colt, grabs Chats's head and calmly walks away, leaving a chill in the air and an O negative spitting neck-fountain on the court. All televised on the Jumbotron above.

The crew is shell-shocked, disbelief so thick you could bite it.

All except Leon. He looks around. Sees Pike. Sees Patience.

"Where's Rasnick?"

18

Rasnick moves with life-threatening urgency through the house, knowing that he has to find that money and quick. In a perfect world, he would find the stash before his brothers got there and be ready to load up and slip out when they arrive, while Leon and company distract that maniac who owns this manor.

He tracks his weapon over the sprawling area he's entered, a space dedicated to Big Ugly's surprising dedication to art and culture. The room is peppered with marvelous ancient stone sculptures of Greek Gods in exile, along with a rich collection of Buddhist artifacts from Indonesia. Rare, eclectic collections of paintings are hung up and down the walls: Botticelli, Vermeer, Whistler, Munch, Dali, Warhol…and a photo of Jenna Jameson autographed in lipstick.

Rasnick tosses a Warhol Big Electric Chair, checking the wall behind it. He pushes at the wall seeking out a secret door. *There's got to be something.* He finds nothing. *Where's the fucking money?*

Rasnick tries another wall.

Flicks the balls of a Hermes statue.

Getting Ugly

He utters an adrenaline-fueled whisper to himself. "Come on. Come on…" Stepping back, he bumps into Chats's head. It has been mounted on the wall—right next to a Pollock that looks like a yak vomited up a bag of Skittles—like a hunting prize in Big Ugly's collection..

Rasnick leaps from his skin. His face drains pale, just shy of translucent. There's a row of ten other heads displayed just like Chats's.

"Fuck!" Rasnick fights to pull it together.

He works to control his breathing as he looks into Chats's dead eyes, thinks about the kind of man Chats was. He was a coldblooded killer, a crazed fighter. Basically, he was a bad motherfucker. If Big Ugly took him down, what the hell is he going to do to Rasnick? He knows he can't afford to think this way. He's here on a mission of commerce and must stay focused. This is about dollars, not dick size.

Rasnick swallows his fear. *You're bad man. Anybody can be gotten to. Big Ugly just got the jump on Chats, that's all. You got to move on.*

He squeezes his GPS Beretta. "Where the hell are they?

19

The sun slips down for the day, framing the mega mansion in a warm, purple glow. The rain has slowed to a peaceful rate, falling gently on the woods. The soft pat, pat of drops landing on leaves gives the lull of a sleepy hideaway.

A vulture yanks and gnaws at the insides of a dead cow.

Zwips whisper-blast the feathered fucker.

Out from the woods step Buster and Talley, officially joining the party. They're dressed head to toe in black SWAT tactical gear: urban assault body armor, laser-sighted modified assault rifles, Glocks, riot helmets with steel grid face shields and cervical neck protectors. The light rain picks up, pissing down on them.

They survey the mess, the carnage-laden wasteland that is Big Ugly's front yard. Soil cut up by landmines, smoldering cow remains, what's left of Oleg and Vig. It's a form of repulsive yard art, cold, hard indicators of what has happened

"Holy hell!" blurts Talley.

Buster snickers, "Fuckin' dope, man."

Talley looks at his brother with disgust.

Buster doesn't get his moods. "What, bro?"

Getting Ugly

"Do you remember the day you became a fucking idiot?"

"Dude, easy…"

"Was it cold that day? Sunny?"

"Asking you, go easy. Please."

"No really? When was it?"

Buster's eyes well. "Begging you…"

"Is it something I did?" asks Talley.

Angry tears form from Buster. "Now I'm warning you."

Talley keeps at it. "If I did, I want to apologize. I'm sorry for assisting you in your quest to become a complete fucking idiot."

"Goddammit, Talley! Lay off me. I'm a person. If you can't accept who I am then…then…I don't fucking know what, but will you please stop judging and accept me like a brother, you complete fucking asshole?"

Talley starts to retort, but stops himself when he sees his brother's hurt expression. Buster wipes away the tears. They stand silent, observing a moment of brotherly reflection.

"Done?" Talley asks.

Buster snorts. "Yes."

Talley nods.

They trudge toward the mega mansion without making eye contact.

20

Leon, Pike, and Patience check each door along a long hallway carpeted in thick red shag.

Leon half expects to see twin girls and something about *Red Rum*. They push on, guns at the ready as they perform a room-to-room sweep. Leon flings open the first door. They find what can only be described as an artillery room, packed wall-to-wall with weapons, ammo, and explosives. Leon thinks he sees a trident in the corner; maybe it's a pitchfork. He motions to the others that it's clear.

Something bothers Pike. "That prick Rasnick went after the money on his own, didn't he?"

Patience seethes.

Leon knows he's right, but they have to stay on task. "Greed's a bitch. Keep your damn voice down." He throws open another door, finding an empty spa-like bathroom. Scans the area. Clear.

Patience looks to Leon. "That your big plan? Dash with cash?"

Leon doesn't answer, thinking, *It's not the worst idea.*

Pike chimes in. "It's always about the money, my man."

"I have other goals, my man," says Leon.

Patience's voice goes soft. "Do tell. What's this all about to you?"

Leon readies himself at the next door. "Not important."

Pike senses his woman's interest in Leon. "If the man don't wanna talk, he don't wanna talk."

Patience zeroes in on Leon, trying to strip away at his defenses with her ample sexuality. It's an effective strategy that's served her well. "Come on Leon, give it up," she purrs.

Leon looks at her. For a second she seems like a human being, an actual real, caring female. Her green eyes glow. "C'mon. Please?" Leon is a strong, disciplined man, but he *is* a still a man, and men can be weaker than shit. It's nature. The basic heterosexual need for female attention fueled by the primitive need to procreate. Not to mention, it's been awhile since a woman gave Leon the time of day, let alone acted like she wanted to hump him.

Leon gets lost her gaze as he explains, "It's about taking back what was taken from me. Finding something positive in all this bad. I lost everything to that man, a life and a woman I loved more than anything. I can never get it all back; I've been reduced to next to nothing. So now, I guess, it's all about just getting back to good."

Pike and Patience actually look moved by his honesty.

Patience takes Leon's face in her hands. "That's best reason I've heard yet. I'm sorry you've been hurt, you gorgeous man." She gently caresses his cheek with the tips of her fingers then whispers, "But you're a complete pussy."

Pike and Patience roll with laughter.

Leon moves on.

Why do I bother?

21

Rasnick moves through an area of the house that looks like a luxury hotel lobby was picked up and dropped directly into the mansion. Brass fixtures, wall-to-wall hardwood floors, and antique furniture placed around the room with perfect symmetry.

Rasnick scans the open space for signs of where the money could be hidden, as well as signs of a crazy fucker trying to kill him. There's an elevator at the far end of the room, with an open stairway next to it. Various doors lead everywhere, as if the room is the connector to the various arteries of the house.

Back in the red shag hallway, Pike and Patience are still giggling. Leon is pissed but hides it fairly well. "Can we?" He gestures down the hallway.

Leon throws open the next door, which leads into a swinger's style love shack equipped with mirrored walls and ceiling. An Olympic-size bed takes up half the room. A sex swing hangs in the center of the room. Leather hoods, whips…you name it line the far wall. It's as if Hustler threw up in here.

Pike and Patience step in. One would think this would be Toys"R"Us to these two. She pushes the sex swing. "Gross." Pike nods in complete agreement. The two of look around, disgusted by what they see. Patience looks at her man and asks, "Since when is that making love?" Leon can only stare in utter disbelief.

The lights go out.

Complete darkness.

Pike barks out, "Cocksucker."

"Take it easy." Urges Leon.

Rasnick is also now in complete darkness. Can't see a damn thing save for the few shards of streaking lightning firing off outside, flickering, flashing, and bouncing light off the polished floor. Rasnick clicks on his tactical flashlight, illuminating the wood paneling that lines the walls of the room.

Just off his left shoulder, he hears the sound of a door opening.

Rasnick fumbles, quickly shutting off the flashlight plunging the lobby into darkness again. A lightning strike cuts the blackness just for a moment, followed by the roll of rumbling thunder. Rasnick presses himself against the wall trying to become invisible.

A shadowy figure slips through the darkness.

Big Ugly.

Rasnick watches, holding his breath, gulping to keep his pounding heart out of his throat. Every part of his being is taut, trying to hide as pure evil walks past. Rasnick pushes harder against the wall. The wall gives a click.

Rasnick's cells freeze.

Big Ugly stops in front of the elevator doors, scans the darkness.

Flipping on the laser sight on his Colt, Big Ugly looks around the room. The red beam carves through the darkness. The wall behind Rasnick has actually opened up revealing a secret door. Rasnick slides through as quickly and quietly as possible, closing the door just a fraction of a second before Big Ugly's laser sight scans over the wall.

In the secret room is nothing but black in every direction. He can't make out where he is.

Rasnick listens closely outside, praying to a merciful God that Big Ugly does not find him.

Big Ugly sweeps his laser sight around the room again. Pauses. Listens closely. Once satisfied there's nothing there, he moves on.

Rasnick listens. *Sounds like he's gone*. He allows himself to breath again. Hopes he didn't piss himself. He clicks his flashlight on, revealing a steep concrete stairway leading down to a steel door at the bottom. He moves down the stairs toward to the door. Readies his weapon, takes a deep breath, yanks the door open.

Pitch black.

Rasnick sweeps the room with his flashlight, stopping as the light illuminates something. He can't make out what it is, but it's something displayed on a small pedestal. A display case of some kind. It's damn peculiar.

Rasnick's jaw goes slack as the contents of the case finally register.

"What the fuck?"

PART IV

Patience, wait!

22

Leon, Pike and Patience are still in darkness. Patience breaks the silence. "Not loving this shit."

Leon keeps his voice calm and flat. "Hold it together. I got a flashlight here, somewhere…"

There's a thick slap of flesh, a crack of bone followed by a muffled yell trailing off into the darkness. Then nothing. Not a sound. Only a bone-chilling silence.

"What the hell happened?" Patience frantically asks.

"I don't know," says Leon.

Thunder crackles.

Fear splits Patience in two. "Baby doll?"

Nothing.

Patience's voice shakes. "Baby?"

"Pike?" calls Leon.

The lights kick back on.

Patience and Leon are all alone among the perverse tools and sexual aids. No Pike. A rippling wave of panic pours over Patience. "Where is he? Where the fuck is he?"

Leon spins, checking all the angles of the room. "I don't know."

Patience spits out the only question that matters. "What did that fucker do to him?"

"We'll find him."

"If he even thinks about hurting him, I'll kill him. I will fucking…" She suddenly stops raging as a cold shard fires up her spine. Her eyes have found a trickle of blood leading out the door. Leon sees it. *Shit*. He tires to put a soothing hand on her but she throws it aside.

"Patience, I know what you're thinking, but we have to be careful here. He wants us to get pissed, get emotional, and make a mistake. This is what he does. Please hear what I'm saying," Leon pleads.

Patience lights caution on fire, pisses on its ashes. She throws open the door. In the hallway, the blood trail snakes down the thick red shag carpet to a door at the far end. The blood is just enough of a shade off the carpet's red to be easily seen. Patience races at full speed, Leon chasing behind her trying to keep up. With guns drawn she flings the door open and rushes through, Leon trailing.

They find themselves in the elevator lobby, now fully lit. The blood trail runs across the hardwood floor, ending in front of the elevator doors.

Leon and Patience aren't allowed time to process information, not given the luxury of time to think. Not even a single second for Leon to try and talk Patience off the ledge.

The elevator dings.

It's coming down.

Patience's breathing becomes low and controlled, her delicate balance of love and hate pulsing. Her emotional levels are spiking beyond normal comprehension.

She commands Leon, "Be. Fucking. Ready."

Leon looks on. *Yes, ma'am*. He tightens his grip on the AR-15, taking aim on the elevator doors. Patience has her

Getting Ugly

M4 ready to rock, rage rippling under her skin. It's hard to contain but she keeps a steady hand, aim dialed in.

Ding.

It's as if the air is sucked out of the room. Nerves are pulled taut. Waiting. The seconds tick away, seeming to last forever. Finally, the elevator doors spread open.

Blood pours out from the elevator like a wild river spreading across the marble floor, covering it. It's as if gallons of dark red paint had been dumped out.

Patience and Leon double-blink, jumping back to avoid the crimson wave. Leon fears the worst. Patience is already there. Her body tremors with anger as if volts of electricity were coursing through her.

Pike's body slips out of the elevator, sliding out on a wave of his own blood. He has been cut open from neck to nuts.

Patience goes apeshit. It's a Titanic-size crush of psychosis that most chemically balanced people will never know, and never should.

From the elevator steps Big Ugly. Leon's pupils flare with hate.

Big Ugly blows Patience a kiss.

All.

Hell.

Breaks.

Loose.

Leon opens up, spewing bursts of AR fire at the elevator. Obliterating pillars. Sending fistfuls of marble flying. Big Ugly returns fire with thumping blasts from his Colt.

Bullets? Not personal enough for Patience. She needs to, has to, must kill Big Ugly with her bare hands. She runs screaming with the finesse of a rabid boar toward Big Ugly, bare feet sloshing through the blood-drenched floor. Big Ugly keeps laying down firepower to keep Leon at bay. He turns his Colt to Patience at the last second, but not before she lunges on him. She wraps her hands around his throat with the force of a sledgehammer shot from a cannon, the collision sending them both hurtling backward into the elevator.

Leon yells, "Patience, wait!"

The doors shut. Elevator dings. Leon is left in the lobby alone with the pools of blood and Pike's corpse. He races to the stairway next to the elevator.

In the elevator rages an all-out war.

Combat in a tight, confined space.

If you took two orangutans, fed them cocaine, then dumped them in an elevator with weapons, this would be the result. Unseemly violence. No style points awarded here. Patience alternates lightning fast jabs to every part of Big Ugly she can hit, unleashing an avalanche of hurt.

Big Ugly gets a good grip on her and tosses her against the opposite wall. He pulls his Colt. Patience springs up with mouth wide, biting down hard on his hand. Blood drips from her lips. Big Ugly pulls back, but her jaw is locked. His Colt drops.

At the stairway, Leon takes the stairs on two, three at a time racing to meet the elevator.

Big Ugly tears Patience's jaws from his hand, but not before she takes some skin and meat with her. Blood smears across her pretty face.

Ding.

Getting Ugly

The door opens. Patience grabs the Colt. Big Ugly's eyes go wide and he blurs out the door as Patience fires with reckless abandon.

Big Ugly spins out into the hall, only to be met by multiple shots snaking up the carpet toward him from Leon's AR. Big Ugly flips a tactical blade at Leon, planting it in his leg. A high velocity splash of blood flies as Leon drops to a knee with a yelp.

Big Ugly makes a jolting leap back into the elevator, ducking Patience's wild, emotional gun blasts.

Leon wails as he pulls the knife from his thigh, the blade taking a piece of him with it.

The sounds of muted, ultra-violent insanity echo from inside the closed elevator.

Ding.

Doors open.

Out comes Big Ugly with Patience attached to him. She faces him, legs wrapped tight around his waist. She has one of her thumbs dug into his eye socket as she fights to angle the Colt with her free hand. She can't get a good shot, but that doesn't stop her. A blast fires off harmlessly, missing Big Ugly's face completely.

Big Ugly wobble-walks through the lobby while fighting and pulling her hands away the best he can. They make their way to the mansion's kitchen, a magnificent room built for gourmets to lust over. Over an island hangs a rack of pots and pans above a butcher's block of ceramic knives.

Outside the door are the sounds of the storm, along with a pack of dogs going berserk. They bark and howl, paws clawing at the door.

Big Ugly can't get Patience off of him. She wails and swipes her long black nails at his face, head and neck with a terrifying level of persistence. She jams the Colt to the top of his head but he swats it away. The stray bullet blows out the sink, water spraying into the air. Big Ugly's hands grab, reaching for anything he can find. His fingers fumble, finding the handle to a hanging pot. He whips it around.

A dull fwap of Calphalon slaps Patience's face, sending her skidding across the tile. Big Ugly yanks a massive ceramic knife from the island. He turns, only to be met by a double blast from his own Colt courtesy of Patience, who is laid out flat on her back. Both shots pound his chest, the brutal force sending him over the kitchen island.

Dogs still bark their balls off from outside.

Lightning fires off.

Patience gets to her feet; she knows damn well he's got a vest on. She steps around the island, her back to an open steel door that leads to a huge Sub-Zero walk-in freezer.

Thunk.

The handle of the ceramic knife bobs from her chest.

A gift courtesy of Big Ugly. Most MLB catchers couldn't make that throw from their knees. Patience's expression drifts to a remote place in the universe, a place far from this kitchen. Her hand releases the Colt, letting it bounce to the tile.

Big Ugly gets to his feet, his ballistic vest now visible through the bullet holes in his exquisite silk shirt. Patience shakes. She summons her remaining shreds of rage as she stumbles toward Big Ugly. Big Ugly pulls another knife from the block, plunging the blade in her stomach with another expert-level throw. He takes a moment to acknowledge how good he is.

The dogs outside continue barking through a storm that is gaining strength.

Patience makes a bounce backward toward the walk-in freezer, but does not go down. Will not go down. She pulls a hidden .38 from under her dress, firing as she lets loose her last death yell.

Big Ugly ducks, spinning toward the back door. He throws the door open to a mad rush of rabid Rottweilers and Dobermans. They leap on Patience with jaws spread wide, the pile of dogs and crazy woman falling back into the walk-in freezer. Big Ugly slams the freezer door shut.

Chewing.

Gnawing.

Tearing.

A few gun shots.

Extremely unpleasant sounds echo and bump from inside the freezer. Big Ugly fixes his hair and adjusts his tie, vanity still on the job.

"Uppity bitch," grunts Big Ugly. He picks up his Colt. Peels a banana on his way out the back door.

The storm rages on.

23

Buster and Talley clear a six lane bowling alley with their SWAT proficiency, pausing at the rumbling sound of distant barking.

"Dogs?" Talley asks.

Buster stands still, staring mesmerized by the porn blazing on the hanging HD screens. Wrinkles his nose. "Dude, I have this one."

"Move," says Talley.

"You think those girls are like, ya know, down–to–earth and shit? Can they talk about things, ya know? Life or whateverthefuck. Anything other than penetration and semen?"

Talley can't look at him.

"What? Seriously. If we're gonna have this kinda jingle in our pockets, we're gonna attract these type of ladies so, therefore, I need to know these type of ladies, right?"

Talley puts up a finger for silence. *For the love of sweet Christ, silence.*

Buster pulls back, hurt. "Rude, dog. You're improving your delivery, slightly, but still flat-out fucking rude."

They reach a door and move into the elevator lobby. Talley and Buster sweep the room, stopping at the river of Pike's blood that's spread across the floor.

"Jesus," Buster says.

A muffled yell.

Buster and Talley spin around, fingers on triggers. It sounds like a voice is coming from inside the wall. Stranger still, it sounded like their brother. Buster and Talley look to each other. *No way.*

The secret doorway cracks open just a bit. Buster and Talley ready their guns. Their brother peaks his head out.

"About motherfuckin' time," Rasnick whisper-yells.

"What the hell is going on here?" asks Talley.

"Don't ask. We need to get gone. C'mon. I've got two bags loaded, but there's a shitload of cash and you won't believe…"

"Hello." Leon limps down the stairs, favoring his leg with the gash. He keeps his AR alternating between the three brothers.

Buster and Talley whip guns around on Leon.

"Who are you?" asks Leon.

"Cleaning ladies," snorts Buster.

"You're cops," says Leon. He looks at Rasnick. "Criminals don't sweep rooms like you."

"Watch a lot of TV," offers Rasnick.

"Who is this clown?" asks Talley.

"I'm former FBI."

Buster rubs the trigger. "He's a lyin' little bitch."

"You think I'm lying, Rasnick?" asks Leon.

Rasnick isn't sure. Eyes lock all around.

"You guys can have the money. I could give a shit less. I'm here to kill Big Ugly and find something for somebody."

Rasnick motions to the open secret door. "Think I found the *something*, but if the *somebody* is the FBI? We've got issues."

"It's got nothing to do with you, man," says Leon.

"The fuck it doesn't," barks Talley.

"You think we can take the money and let you roll up to the F-B-fucking-I?" asks Buster.

"I won't tell a soul."

"Fucking well right you won't," cracks Buster.

Tension high. Three guns on Leon against his one. Fingers itch on triggers. Then…

A goat walks across the floor.

Big silence.

A strange pause in this Mexican standoff as Big Ugly's "friend" trots across the bloody floor. The goat clears the room, on its way to the kitchen. Eyes bounce among the four men. Talley looks to Rasnick. "Call it, man."

Leon knows the answer before it's said.

"Kill him," says Rasnick.

A wave of bullets plow toward Leon. He returns fire with his AR, pumping rapid bursts, but the firepower coming from the other side is a monster. Talley sidesteps while firing, getting a new angle. His foot slips on the slick blood that coats the hardwood, causing his legs to fly out from under him. His finger involuntarily squeezes the trigger as his legs fold. As he lands, the stray bullet-spray carves up his neck and face, the barrel landing on his temple for the final kill shot.

Talley's body flops to the floor.

Rasnick hasn't noticed and keeps up the pounding fire on Leon, pushing Leon out of the room. Buster's brain circuits crossfire with overloading emotions, his head a synaptic car fire.

Leon skids into a room filled with a jaw-dropping display of flowers and plants, birds flying above a sanctuary that is complete with a retractable glass roof that is currently closed. The rain pours down through the moonlight, providing a drum solo rhythm on the glass. Leon reloads, limping his way through the massive, Garden of Eden area.

In the elevator lobby, Rasnick lumbers catatonic over to Buster, who stands over their dead brother neither of them knows exactly what happened. Buster is a frantic, mumbling mess. "Fucking shit."

"You killed Talley?" asks Rasnick.

"What?"

"You were his primary backup and you failed him."

Buster's mind scrambles, no idea how to respond to his brother's analysis of the situation. "I didn't mean to dog. He was repositioning and I...I...I..."

"You may as well have shot our brother."

Buster swallows hard. "Oh come on, man..."

"You always hated him."

"Not true. Take that shit back. Unfucking true..."

"Bullshit! From day one, you never liked him."

"We had differences for sure, but not like this."

"The Green Machine incident of 1985?"

Buster's eyes moisten. "You gonna throw that in my face? Now, asshole, at a time like this?"

A whistle sounds out from across the room. Buster and Rasnick swivel. Rasnick squints at a man cloaked in shadow.

Buster asks, "Who the fuck are you?"

Rasnick knows. He raises his weapon in an attempt to take down the devil.

A second splits in two.

Buster and Rasnick are each met by a single bullet to the brain. They flop in a heap next to their brother.

24

Leon scramble-limps though the doors of an indoor water haven that destroys even the best Cancun party pools. That kick-ass cement pond you saw on Cribs a few years ago? Bullshit compared to this. BIG UGLY is etched in gold, centered perfectly under the rippling water of the gargantuan pool. A raging waterfall lies at the far end, with rock cliffs designed for diving. The retractable glass roof that began in the garden room stretches into this room.

Leon holds his seeping knife wound. The blood doesn't show too badly through his black REI cargos, just looks like he's pissed himself—perhaps the only time in his life that Leon wishes that was really the case.

He looks up.

The glass roof has begun to retract, opening up and allowing the rain to dump down. The driving rain pounds Leon. The thunder and lightning dance in the moonlight, providing the mood for his perfect little reunion with…

Big Ugly.

In steps the world's leading producer of misery, the master of disaster.

He stands on the cliff just behind the waterfall, taking a stance like the God of War—at least in his mind. Slightly battered from his battles with his various guests, but he knows he's still the goods. The waterfall parts like curtains for him as he steps forward. A samurai sword is sheathed behind his back, a Colt tucked into his lizard skin belt.

Leon's face goes slack. The object of his personal demise stands a mere pool length away. The man who ruined his existence on this planet, who killed his dreams and pissed on his soul. Leon's very DNA burns. His face darkens, hate pushing the needle to the point of mental implosion.

Big Ugly grins wide. "Leon."

"Big Ugly."

"Been awhile."

"Too long."

Big Ugly cocks his head birdlike. "You look like shit, buddy." Leon flashes a fake smile. Big Ugly keeps pushing buttons. "How's your ass? Heard you needed stitches. Were there stitches?"

Leon drops the smile.

"I get it confused. If you're sodomized by a guy wearing a strap-on, does that make you gay? Or is the guy wearing the strap-on gay? I don't feel gay. Do you feel gay, Leon?"

Leon grips his AR.

Big Ugly cracks his knuckles. *Show time.*

Leon can't hold back any longer. He unleashes years worth of hostility, unloading hyper-burst of relentless lead. With Olympic precision, Big Ugly dives into the pool with very little splash. He cuts underwater like a jet-propelled merman.

Leon continues firing round after round into the pool. He pulls back seeing no sign of Big Ugly. He holds his fire, conserving his ammo. The ripples in the water fade. Only the plops of heavy rain churn the pool as the storm continues to pour down from the dark skies above.

Lightning flashes.

Thunder cracks.

From the dark water springs Big Ugly, swiping his sword at Leon's legs. Leon hops, the blade barely missing as he fights to take aim on Big Ugly. Before he can get a shot off, Big Ugly whips the sword around cutting the AR in half. Leon drops what's left of weapon to the tile. Big Ugly leaps from the pool, sword poised for mutilation. Leon tosses a deck chair with everything he has, slipping and sliding trying to make his way to an exit.

Big Ugly dodges the chair with minimal effort. Leon grabs another chair, letting it fly. Big Ugly cuts it into a non-threat. Leon trips over a fallen table. Big Ugly's sword comes slicing down. Leon rolls, the blade sparking off the tile. Leon lands a foot to Big Ugly's face, giving him enough of an opening to bolt to for the door.

Leon stumbles through, landing outside the house. Squinting through the driving rain, he realizes he's entered an MLB level batting cage. He gets to his feet and backs away from the door, waiting, anticipating, Big Ugly's arrival.

Fwoomp.

A baseball tags him square in the ribs. Leon feels an internal crunch of bone which robs the air from his lungs.

Fwoomp.

Another ball nails his thigh, taking his leg out from under him. Big Ugly charges through the door like an insane Apache, plunging the sword at Leon's face. He dodges hard left; the blade misses his ear by an inch.

Leon falls back, his fingers finding a Louisville Slugger. He slams it into Big Ugly's nuts.

Gut.

Face.

Big Ugly stumbles from side to side, swallowing back the snot and blood. He fights to clear his vision while tremors rocket from his groin to his feet. He staggers toward a cage door that leads back into the house. Fastballs whizz around them. Some miss. Some don't. Big Ugly swings his sword with one hand, trying to hold back the blood pouring from his nose with his free hand. He cuts a ball in half.

Leon swings his bat. Big Ugly dodges, returning with a quick jab to Leon's eye. Leon whips his bat around. Big Ugly can't get a full swipe, but gets in position enough to block the blow with his blade. The sword and bat lock together, sword stuck deep into the wood. They tug and pull, tumbling back through the door into elevator lobby. They've entered the now familiar room from the opposite side.

War rages.

Punches rock.

They are engaged in full-on brutality as they fight to free the sword from the bat. Behind their struggle, the heavy coating of blood spreads across the slick floor glistening in the moonlight. The secret door Rasnick found is wide open.

Leon spots the door just over Big Ugly's shoulder, catching a glimpse of the stairs leading down. He glances down to the Colt still in Big Ugly's belt. Leon pumps the sword/bat combo hard into Big Ugly's face.

Once.

Twice.

Three times.

Big Ugly's face busts to shit. His eyes glaze over, his equilibrium thrown off. The sword/bat hits the floor. Leon rears back then bull-rushes, ramming a shoulder hard into Big Ugly like a runaway train striking a tackling dummy. The tangled pair hit the blood-soaked marble at ramming speed, gliding along the blood while tracking a straight line directly toward the secret doorway.

They rip through the door and down the stairs like riding a horrific Slip 'N Slide.

PART V
Chester

25

An angry tumbleweed of humanity screams down the stairs.

A shard of light from the open door cuts through the dark, perfectly framing the pile of Big Ugly and Leon. A mutated mess of arms, legs and hate barrels through, skidding to a stop leaving them in an inert lump on the cold floor.

Leon peels off, wobbling to find his balance. "Do not fucking move." Leon has managed to get his hands on the Colt during the tumble. He holds it dead on Big Ugly.

Big Ugly is laid out on the floor in a somewhat broken, blood-soaked pile. It's been a damn rough day. Leon wipes blood from his face and feels around for a way to get the lights on.

Leon's eyes pop. "Son of a bitch."

As the room lights up he realizes he's in a room full of money. A vault made for kings. Leon can't help but think of when Bugs and Daffy found the genie's treasure. Stacks of hundreds reach for the ceiling. All the money Big Ugly has taken over the years. The sum of all his labor, his big score. Leon takes a moment to drink it all in. On the floor are two cash-stuffed Nike bags—the ones Rasnick never got a chance to come back to. Big Ugly regards the bags. "Movies make people stupid. Million dollars weighs about twenty pounds. You can't carry two thousand pounds in two fucking bags."

"Where is it?" Leon asks.

Big Ugly spits out a tooth. "Where's what, love?"

Leon spins around looking. "Where's the video, the records, the files. Whatever you have that is keeping you safe?"

"Oh. You mean, Chester."

Leon looks to him. *Chester?*

Big Ugly motions behind him. Just over his right shoulder is a small platform lit with a warm glow. This is what Rasnick saw.

Leon is dumbstruck. "You've got to be kidding me."

Displayed like the Mona Lisa in a sealed glass case, lit by a beam overhead, is a gargantuan dildo. Big Ugly grins ear-to-ear. "Had some people put the display together. Vacuum sealed to lock in dead hooker DNA and keep fingerprints crystal clear and incriminating as shit, the way God intended them to be."

Leon's mind spins trying to piece together what this could possibly mean. His thoughts come together, only to explode into insane theories. He attempts to work this mental Silly Putty into some form logic. "Senators and Supreme Court judges were mixed up with call girls and you had this? That thing?"

"Who?" asks Big Ugly.

Leon starts over. "Senators. Judges. They don't want you to give that over to the authorities."

"What the fuck are you talking about, Nature Boy?"

A gun clicks.

A familiar voice speaks.

"Love to have that dildo, son."

26

Leon spins around to find Cooper holding a 9mm in each hand, the right one for Leon, the left for Big Ugly.

Leon, mouth agape, struggles to find the best word. "Fucker."

"All the guns and goodies I gave you were bugged with tracking devices," says Cooper.

Leon levels a death stare that sears through his onetime hero slash father figure. His current hate object.

"Sorry, kid. I am a lifer, dedicated to God, country and all that. Believe me, I had every intention of brining that son of a bitch to justice when I recruited you. Truly did. But I've got weaknesses, like everybody else. I like the hookers."

"Who doesn't?" adds Big Ugly. Cooper plants a shoe to his gut and Big Ugly coughs up some blood with a giggle.

Cooper explains, "This prick got to me while you were in Mexico." Cooper leans down to Big Ugly. "You really didn't have to kill all the girls."

"Yeah, kinda did. See, that's what makes Chester so sweet, like pumpkin pie. He gives the impression you killed the skanks. Get it?"

Getting Ugly

Cooper kicks him again. Harder.

"You understand," coughs Big Ugly.

Leon's mind churns. "You were the lead on his case. You asked me to go after him, and then when he got dirt on you you sold me out, made all the charges, all intelligence just simply go away?"

"Yes, yes I did."

Leon explodes, "You fucking piece of shit!"

"Be that as it may."

"You two need a moment?" asks Big Ugly.

"Shut that goddam mouth," barks Cooper.

Leon's guts twist like bread ties. An all too familiar feeling to Leon, that same old feeling that can only come from the being the last to know you've been completely fucked over. "I wanted to be a good agent —get it right, live a life to be proud of." Leon's eyes glaze over. "You people, you fucking people used me up and shit on what was left."

"Yeah, kid. I'm gonna need that dildo," says Cooper dismissively.

Big Ugly slow rolls into laughter. Cooper joins the joke with a snicker. He knows it's not funny, but there's something about joining in on a joke that's irresistible, a *thank God I'm not that guy* sort of thing.

Leon is not remotely amused.

Vibrates with anger.

Blam!

Leon fires a single bullet between Cooper's eyes. A jet of red pulp shoots across the Nike bags as his body drops. Even Big Ugly is surprised. Leon turns the Colt on him.

Big Ugly springs.

Blam!

Leon's stray shot misses Big Ugly, but shatters the glass case. Chester wiggles free and flops to the concrete.

Big Ugly's head fires up like a piston, pulverizing Leon's chin from below. The Colt skips across the floor and Leon falls as Big Ugly bolts for a back door. Big Ugly hauls ass, retreating beyond the stacks of cash.

Leon's fingers scramble and claw for something, anything. He finds Chester. He hums it with everything he has. Chester catches Big Ugly on the ankle, just enough to trip him up. Big Ugly hits the floor, skidding into the library.

Leon launches into the air, landing on top of Big Ugly. Big Ugly flips around, throwing Leon, who sails over a leather couch. He comes up grabbing for a lamp, which he smashes on Big Ugly's head. Leon grabs a book from a towering bookcase and slams the spine into Big Ugly's face. Big Ugly counters by flipping a coffee table up and jamming the edge into Leon's throat.

Punches land with a constant smack of flesh. Kicks miss, then hit. Bones crunch. Ligaments tear as limbs twist. Blood spits and spills on the fine Persian rugs. It's a brawl of biblical proportions.

The thing that separates them, gives Leon the edge, is that Leon fucking hates Big Ugly, while Big Ugly just wants to fight. Leon is driven beyond reason. His blood burns hot, the needle passed rage a long time ago. Leon pushes himself to another level of violence, a new emotion that is yet to be defined.

He beats Big Ugly with a left, then a right. Throws a hammer kick sending Big Ugly hard against a far wall covered with large velvet curtains. Something behind the curtains gives an odd crunch; there's glass behind it. Could be windows, not sure.

Leon comes at him, a man possessed, kicks and punches thrown with every ounce of his being. Big Ugly can barely defend himself from the blitz of hand-to-hand hell. With every blow the glass behind Big Ugly crunches a little more. Leon grabs Big Ugly's neck, spit flying from his lips as he slams Big Ugly's head repeatedly against the glass until…

Crash.

They tumble through the shattered glass, hurtling and smashing into a new room as the busted glass showers the floor. They land in a pile, bouncing on the white tile with Leon on top riding Big Ugly to a jolting stop.

Leon finds his feet. Big Ugly leans forward, resting on his elbows. He's bloodied, his face a mess, but still manages a smile. Leon pulls the Colt, poking Big Ugly in the eye with the barrel. It's similar to the scene in Mexico when Big Ugly had the jump on Leon, but things have changed.

"Hola, my little Fed friend," says Big Ugly.

"Hi," says Leon, seething. He fights to control his breathing and pounding heart.

"Seriously, when are you going cease with the shit?"

Leon pulls back the hammer. "Thinking today's the day." Leon stops, thrown by Big Ugly's expression—he almost appears happy. *Wants to be shot?*

Big Ugly says, "I wanted it to be you, but you had to earn it. Couldn't just give it to you."

Leon scans the area. They've landed in a room that looks like a high-end hospital room via W Hotel. There's a king-size adjustable bed, glass cases lined with prescription bottles, syringes, blood tests…way too much medical equipment for the average human being.

Leon gets it. "You're sick."

"Understatement of the year."

"What's with the private hospital?"

"My body's a temple."

Leon inspects some of the drug bottles. "These aren't TUMS. This is serious medication. What do you have? Cancer? What?"

"Oh, it's some nasty, nasty shit," sneers Big Ugly.

Leon spots the handheld surveillance monitor that Big Ugly has been carrying around. It peeks from his suit jacket, strapped to Big Ugly by a shoulder strap. Leon rips it away. He touches the screen, flipping through the different views. On the monitor he sees Chats's headless body on the basketball court. Swipe. The carnage of Pike at the elevators. Then the kitchen, the brothers, the vault with dead Agent Cooper and, finally, the crew's Chevy Suburban and Brobee's Caddie parked on the road outside the woods.

A light bulb goes off for Leon, then explodes. "Nobody gets near here without you knowing about it." Leon mind plays through events, stringing together his thoughts, the stories he's heard, the things he knows. Rearranges them in some form of order in an attempt to apply logic where it has no business being used. In his mind's eye, it starts to play out clear as day.

The country road. Brobee's stolen Caddie running out of gas, sputtering to a stop near the woods. Leon connects the dots. Brobee stumbled onto Big Ugly by accident, but he could've gone in any direction, up or down the road, even stayed at the car.

Getting Ugly

The Office. Big Ugly sitting in his designer suit in front of his sea of security monitors. He spotted the Caddie, saw Brobee get out of the car. Big Ugly's eyes slammed into focus, recognizing. Big Ugly raced down the hall passing his staff and hookers, cigar and scotch still in hand.

Big Ugly storming out the door into the night air, checking his handheld surveillance monitor looking at Brobee. He starts to sing at the top of his lungs, wanting to make sure Brobee comes his way. Brobee walks into the woods. Big smile from Big Ugly.

Back into the mansion, Big Ugly glides through the foyer talking with Bobby. "I know you haven't been yourself," *says Bobby.* "Depression is a natural response."

"Appreciate your concern," *replies Big Ugly.*

Big Ugly moves down the line in the formal dining room handing out stacks of money to his staff. He reaches the Doctor. "I'm not leaving here. You need help."

Big Ugly nods.

Leon eyes flare. "You wanted us to come here." He stands over Big Ugly, holding the Colt at his side. Big Ugly's smile still shines through the blood.

"You wanted one last battle."

"Warriors were made to war, not die in bed."

"You wanted us to kill you, go down in flames."

"C'mon, Leon. Don't pussy out now." Big Ugly grabs Leon's gun hand, directing the Colt at his own face. "You've dreamed of killing me. Pull that trigger. This is it. Do it. Take it. Get some release, man. Nobody's been able to take me out. You can be the one. Conquering FBI hero who got his man."

Big Ugly licks the gun barrel.

Leon is wrapped in complete disbelief. Big Ugly recites an earlier line he used with Bobby. "You know the win/loss record for people who make the big score and retire to the sweet life? One winner and a fucking pissload of losers. I'm the one."

"No, you're not," says Leon with glazed eyes.

"Pardon?"

Leon rips the Colt away from Big Ugly's puzzled face. Safely lowers the hammer. Shoves his hate down with a better idea. "You don't get to win. You don't get to die like a gladiator. No blaze of glory." Big Ugly works another angle, other buttons to push. "Think, boy. Cooper destroyed my records. Feds got nothing on me."

"I know."

"Whatever the fuck Cooper promised you, it died with him."

"You're under arrest."

"You think you can just walk back into your old life? Get fucking real."

He's getting to Leon.

"Maybe not," admits Leon.

"Maybe? Seriously? You're nothing. You're a cum stain on a tranny's skirt."

Leon starts to raise the gun, so Big Ugly pours it on. "I'll be out of lockup before I finish my McMuffin, and once I'm out I'm going to run a killing spree that'll make cancer look like a fun way to check out. I'm a bad man. Baddest motherfucker in the history of bad motherfuckers." Leon whips the butt of the Colt across Big Ugly's jaw, putting him on the floor. Ending Big Ugly's sermon.

Leon leans in close, wants to make sure Big Ugly gets this. "They are going to find you in a house littered with bodies. In particular, three dead cops and an FBI agent. And, oh yeah, millions of unaccounted for dollars that I'll bet my balls isn't on your last tax return. Yeah, I'm pretty sure that'll fuckin' stick, Billy Badass."

Big Ugly's stomach drops farther and farther with every word.

"You get to die in a cage you pathetic, silly cunt." This is the first time Big Ugly's ever had a sliver of fear in his life. Leon is enjoying this moment, the moment he's earned. "First day, they'll probably kick your teeth out so your mouth gives that smooth vagina-like feel."

Big Ugly panics.

A new side to the scariest man alive.

He jumps at Leon. Twisting the Colt away, he jams it under his own chin attempting to shoot himself. Leon pounces on his back, pushing the gun away at the last second. The shot rings out harmlessly as they struggle for control of the gun.

Fighting against Leon's grip, Big Ugly uses every fiber of his being trying to stick the gun in his own mouth, fighting to pull the trigger. Dying to kill himself.

Both their faces burn red. Veins pop. Spit flies. Fingers fumble around the trigger.

Odd change in circumstances, one Leon never could have imagined—him trying to save Big Ugly's life, Big Ugly trying to end it.

Grunts.

Punches.

Profanity.

A gunshot rings out.

Silence…then a crack of thunder.

"Fuck you, Grande Ugly."

27

The clang of steel sliding shut rattles behind Big Ugly as he walks though the maximum security facility. Draped in an orange jumpsuit, his new identity is stenciled neatly above his breast pocket—he's just a number now. His hard gaze burns as the bars slam with that unmistakable sound. No longer the untouchable master of darkness in a ten grand suit, today he's just another guest of the U.S. Correctional System.

In the yard, Big Ugly keeps to himself. Even here he's confident he has no equal and would rather not mix with the local yokels. From behind Big Ugly, a mix of tattoo-skinned, shaved-head felons move toward him, a gleam twinkles in their eyes.

The smallest one is six four, two sixty, and they are not fans seeking an autograph. Big Ugly has only been here a few days and so far he's already killed an inmate, paralyzed two, and sent three guards home for some much needed time for healing and reflection. Some of the prison officials unofficially decided that Big Ugly needed "socialization" with other inmates in order to facilitate a smoother transition. They even went as far as to allow this very group of shaved-head felons some extra shop time in order to create something special for the task.

They huddle in, surrounding Big Ugly.

The Guards look the other way.

Big Ugly turns, facing the pack of hostile inmates he finds a defiant grin. He still holds onto his edge, still able to find just the right thing to say to people.

"Who's fucking first?"

The crazed felons attack.

Big Ugly thinks of Leon.

Leon would enjoy this.

The bluest of water kisses the white sand, sun beaming through the slight, whispering breeze. A gorgeous bikini-clad waitress snakes down the beach of the remote island paradise, delivering a cocktail.

She reaches Leon, who's sprawled out in a chair like a lazy feline. Healing cuts and scars pepper his face and tanning body. His leg is still strapped in a brace, and his arm hangs in a sling from a gunshot wound.

The waitress hands him a towering Bloody Mary with a sexy smile. Leon digs into the tattered Nike bag that rests in the sand next to his chair, pulling a hundred from under the beach towel on top. The waitress takes the bill, pausing as she notices the dried bloodstains.

"Sorry," says Leon as he fumbles around, finding her a clean, fresh hundred. He sips the cocktail as he lies back, waving off the change. The waitress thanks him with a smile, her blonde hair rippling in the ocean breeze.

Leon returns the smile then asks, "You know the win/loss record for people who make the big score and retire to the sweet life? One winner and many, many losers."

She smiles through her confusion. "Que?"

Leon offers a big smile. "I'm the one."

Leon coughs hard.

Wheezes.

Gasps.

His lungs struggle to find a breath through his closing throat.

The waitress giggles and leans down to Leon's ear, speaking perfect English. "Sorry, sweetheart." Leon's eyes bulge as he grabs his throat, panic spiking as his brain starts to process the very real possibility of dropping dead from lack of oxygen.

The waitress kisses his forehead. Leon notices the small black heart tattoo above her right breast. His mind splits in two.

She's the blonde ATV driving hooker!

The last thing Leon sees is the blonde pouring the drink into the sand before picking up his Nike bag. She checks the contents, finding his room key along with various papers and a keychain. She proudly walks down the beach, raising the bag above her head as if showing off a trophy or championship belt for all to see.

Just on the horizon, near the water, the other girl, the brunet ATV hooker, stands with her double Ds muted under a tasteful dress. She waits for her girl with a warm smile. She thinks of the time spent in captivity with Big Ugly. It was a rough time, but today she and her girl get what they've earned. All that weird shit with that monster of a man took its toll, and most of the girls at the mansion relied heavily on the drugs and booze to get them through the endless days and nights with Big Ugly.

Not the brunet and the blonde.

They paid attention.

To everything.

They took note of the details, of the devil performing those details. They watched Big Ugly, how he got information, how he processed that info, how he did his business. It's easy to dismiss two hookers with fake double Ds who spread the dumb girl act on thick as molasses while being used so causally for sex.

Now? Today? It's a much different time.

Their time.

They didn't leave the woods that day. No, after they gave Big Ugly's message to Leon and the crew they hung around. They laid low and paid close attention. They watched Leon kill Cooper and take Big Ugly kicking and screaming to the proper law enforcement authorities. They studied Leon's patterns, tracked the man, picked up the trail that lead them here to this perfect little island paradise.

The blonde reaches her love, Nike bag in hand. She wraps her arm around the brunet's waist. "I've got the key to his room."

"The storage shed?"

"Yup." The blonde dangles the keychain. "Gotta be where he keeps the rest of it."

They get lost in one another's eyes. So much shared between them, so much endured. No words are needed.

The blonde and brunet lock their finger together, holding hands as they walk along the sand watching the waves roll in.

Two winners in a world of so many losers.

Mike McCrary's new crime thriller **REMO WENT ROGUE** is coming soon…

ACKNOWLEDGMENTS

You can't do a damn thing alone, so I'd like to thank the people who gave help and hope during this little fun and self-loathing writing life.

First, thanks to Elmore Leonard, Don Winslow, Stephen King, Chuck Palahniuk, Duane Swierczynski, Charlie Huston and Dennis Lehane. You don't know me, but thank you for what you do. Thanks, in no particular order, to the following writers, bad-asses, good dudes and Book Gods: Blake Crouch, Allan Guthrie, John Rector, Peter Farris, Johnny Shaw and David Hale Smith. Thank you for talking books and the publishing world with me, even if you didn't know you were doing it.

Big, massive, sloppy love to the good folks at MXN Entertainment for never wavering in their help and support over the years. Mason Novick…thank you doesn't cover it, man.

Love and appreciation to my family and friends who have put up with me and my bullshit—you know who are. Thanks to Mom and Dad for not selling me for medical experiments, and last but not least, thank you to my beautiful wife and daughter. You have endured and embraced me during my bitter, cranky, moody and (let's just fuckin' say it) dark days. For that and for everything, every day…I love you.

ABOUT THE AUTHOR

Mike McCrary is a screenwriter who has worked with (or at least been in the same room with) the producers of several movies you've probably heard of, you may or may not have liked them, but you're heard of them. His short fiction has appeared in *Out of the Gutter, Shotgun Honey* and *The Big Adios*.

Mike barely earned an Economics degree, somehow got an MBA, and has been a waiter, securities trader, dishwasher, investment manager, and an unpaid Hollywood intern. He's quit corporate America, come back, been fired, been promoted, been fired, and currently writes stories about questionable people who make questionable decisions. He lives in Texas. Keep up with Mike at www.mikemccrary.com or follow him @mcmccrary.

CPSIA information can be obtained
at www.ICGtesting.com
Printed in the USA
LVHW02s0412211217
560416LV00002B/446/P